CHEMICAL VALLEY

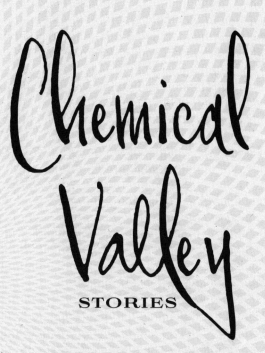

Chemical Valley

STORIES

DAVID HUEBERT

A JOHN METCALF BOOK

BIBLIOASIS
WINDSOR, ONTARIO

FIRST EDITION
10 9 8 7 6 5 4 3 2 1

Library and Archives Canada Cataloguing in Publication

Title: Chemical valley / David Huebert.
Names: Huebert, David, author.
Description: Short stories.
Identifiers: Canadiana (print) 20210213477 | Canadiana (ebook) 20210213507 |
    ISBN 9781771964470 (softcover) | ISBN 9781771964487 (ebook)
Classification: LCC PS8615.U3 C54 2021 | DDC C813/.6—dc23

Edited by John Metcalf
Copyedited by Chandra Wohleber
Text and cover designed by Ingrid Paulson

"Dandelion Wine" written by Gregory Alan Isakov © 2009 Suitcase Town Music
Courtesy of Third Side Music

Published with the generous assistance of the Canada Council for the Arts, which last year invested $153 million to bring the arts to Canadians throughout the country, and the financial support of the Government of Canada. Biblioasis also acknowledges the support of the Ontario Arts Council (OAC), an agency of the Government of Ontario, which last year funded 1,709 individual artists and 1,078 organizations in 204 communities across Ontario, for a total of $52.1 million, and the contribution of the Government of Ontario through the Ontario Book Publishing Tax Credit and Ontario Creates.

PRINTED AND BOUND IN CANADA

For my parents—Ron Huebert and Elizabeth Edwards

In those days the world teemed,
the people multiplied,
the world bellowed like a wild bull.
THE EPIC OF GILGAMESH

Cutting grass for gasoline, for gasoline.
GREGORY ALAN ISAKOV

CONTENTS

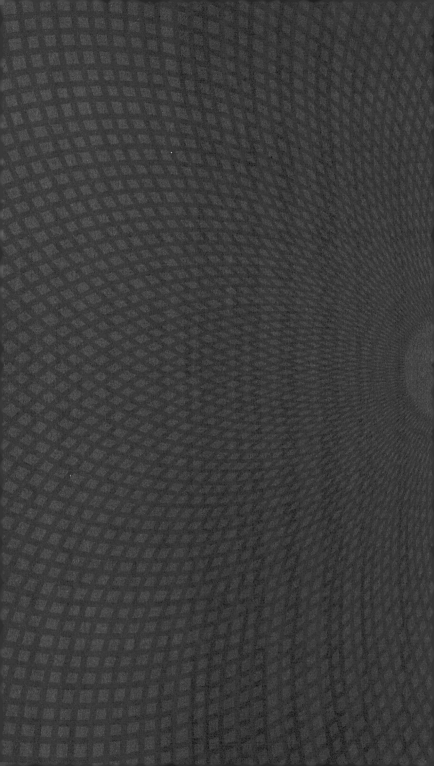

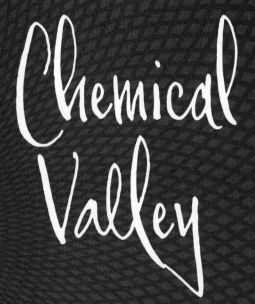

CHEMICAL VALLEY

I KNEEL DOWN and reach for the nearest bird, hydraulics buzzing in my teeth and knees. The pigeon doesn't flinch or blink. No blood. No burn smell. Sal's there in seconds, his face a blear of night-shift grog. He rubs his bigger eye, squats by the carcasses. Behind him the river wends and glimmers, slicks through refinery glare.

"Poison you figure?" Sal thumbs his coverall pockets.

"Leak maybe."

Suzy appears next to Sal, seeping chew-spit into her Coke can. She leans over and takes a pigeon in her Kevlared paw. Brings it to her face. "Freaky," she says, bottom lip bulging. "Eyes still open." She wiggles her rat face into a grin, a frond of tobacco wagging in her bottom teeth.

I can't afford to say it: "Saving that for later?"

Suzy flares: "What?"

"The chew."

Suzy puts a hand over her mouth, speaks with taut lips: "Enough of your guff."

I snort. "Guff?"

She sets the bird down, hitches her coveralls. Lips closed, she tongues the tobacco loose and swallows. "Clean 'em up," she says, nodding at the pigeons. She spins and walks away, trailing chew-spit across the unit.

WHAT YOU MIGHT find, if you were handling a dead pigeon, is something unexpected in the glassy cosmos of its eye: a dark beauty, a molten alchemy. You might find a pigeon's iris looks how you imagine the Earth's core—pebble-glass waves of crimson, a perfect still shudder of rose and lilac. What you might do, if you were placing a dead pigeon into the incinerator, is take off your Kevlar glove and touch your bare index finger to its cornea. What you might do before dropping the bird into a white-hot Mordor of carbon and coke is touch your fingertip to that unblinking membrane and hold it there, feeling a mangle of tenderness and violation, thinking this may be the loveliest secret you have ever touched.

I'M TELLING EILEEN how I want to be buried, namely inside a tree. We're sitting in bed eating Thai from the mall and listening to the 6:00 p.m. construction outside our window—the city tearing up the whole street along with tree roots and a rusted tangle of lead pipes—and I'm telling Eileen it's called a biodegradable burial pod. Mouth full of cashew curry and I'm saying what they do is put your remains in this egg-looking thing like the xenomorph's cocoon from *Alien: Resurrection* but it's made of biodegradable plastic. I'm telling Eileen it's called "capsula mundi" and what they do is hitch the remains to a semi-mature tree and plant the whole package. Stuff you down in fetal position and let you gradually decay until you become nitrogen, seep into soil.

Contemplating panang, Eileen asks where I got the idea about the burial pod and I tell her Facebook or maybe an email newsletter. "You click on that shit? Why are you even thinking about this now? You just turned thirty-four."

I don't tell her about the basement, about Mum. I don't tell her about the pigeons strewn out on the concrete and then going supernova in the incinerator, don't mention how it gets me thinking about flesh, about bodies, about waste. I don't tell her about Blane, the twenty-nine-year-old long-distance runner who got a heart attack sitting at the panel in the Alkylation unit. Blane didn't die but he did need surgery and a pacemaker and that sort of thing gets you curious. Which is how you end up lying in bed at night checking your pulse and feeling like your chest is shrinking and thinking about the margin of irregular and erratic.

Picking a bamboo shoot from her molars: "Since when are you into trees?"

She says it smug. She says it like Miss University Sciences, and nobody else is allowed to like trees. I don't tell her how we're all compost and yes I read that on a Facebook link. I also do not tell her about the article's tag line: "Your carbon footprint doesn't end in the grave." Reaching for the pad Thai, I tell her about the balance, how it's only natural. How the human body's rich in nitrogen, how when you use a coffin there's a lot of waste because the body just rots on its own when it could be giving nutrients to the system. Not to mention all the metals and treated woods in coffins. I tell her how the idea is to phase out traditional graveyards entirely, replace them with grave-forests.

"Hmm," Eileen says, gazing out the window—the sky a caramelized rose. "Is this a guilt thing, from working at the plants?"

I tell her no, maybe, I don't know. An excavator hisses its load into the earth.

"Is this why you were so weird about your mother's funeral?"

I ask what she means and she says never mind, sorry.

"Do you ever imagine they're ducks?"

Eileen asks what and I tell her the loaders and the bull-dozers and the cranes. Sometimes I imagine they're wildlife, ducks or geese. And maybe why they're crying like that is because they're in distress. Like maybe they've lost their eggs and all they want is to get them back and when you think about it like that it's still bad but at least it's not just machines screaming and blaring because they're tearing up old sidewalks to put new ones down.

"Ducks," Eileen says. "Probably still be one working for every three scratching their guts for overtime pay."

She stacks the containers and reaches for the vaporizer on the nightstand, asking if I love trees so much why didn't I become a landscaper or a botanist or an arborist. I shrug, not mentioning the debt or the mortgage or the pharmaceutical bills. Not mentioning that if I wanted to do something it would be the comic store but there's no market in Sarnia anyway.

I tell her it's probably too late for a career change.

"No," she coos, pinching my chin the way I secretly loathe. She smiles her sweet stoned smile, a wisp of non-smoke snaking through her molars. "You could do anything. You could be so much." Eileen lies down on her back on the bed, telling the ceiling I could be so much and the worst part is she means it. The worst and the best all coiled together as I reach out and thumb the curry sauce from her chin, thinking about when she'll fall asleep and I'll drift down to the basement, to Mum.

IN 1971 THE Trudeau government issued a ten-dollar-bill picturing Sarnia's new refinery metropolis as a paean to Canadian progress. Inked in regal purple, the buildings rise up space-aged and triumphant, a *Jetsons* wet dream. Towers jab through the sky and cloudlike drums pepper the ground, a suspended rail line curling around the scene. Smokestacks and ladders and tanks and tubs. Glimmering steel and perfect concrete, a shimmering fairy city and the strange thing is that what you don't see is oil, what you never see is oil. The other strange thing is that this is how Sarnia used to be seen, that not so long ago the plants were shiny and dazzling and now they're rusty with paint peeling off the drums and poor maintenance schedules and regular leaks and weeds all over, stitching concrete seams.

ON THE DRIVE to work a woman on the radio is talking about birth rates as the corn fields whish and whisper. Eileen doesn't know this or need to but I drive the long way to work because I like to pass through the corn fields. What I like about them is the sameness: corn and corn and corn and it makes you think that something is stable, stable and alive and endless, or about as close as you can get. If Eileen was in the car she'd say, "As high as an elephant's eye in July." Then she'd probably say her thing about ethanol. How the nitrogen fertilizer comes from ammonia, which comes from natural gas. How the petrochemical fertilizer is necessary to grow super-huge varieties of hybrid corn products that mostly turn into livestock feed but also a significant portion turns into ethanol. Ethanol that is then used as a biofuel supplement to gasoline so what it is is this whole huge cycle of petroleum running subterranean through modern biological life.

The reporter is saying how first it was the birds and then it was the reserve and now they're getting worried. Now they're seeing plant workers producing only female children. No official studies on the area because Health Canada won't fund them but the anecdotal evidence is mounting and mounting and the whole community knows it's in their bodies, in their intimate organs, zinging through their spit and blood and lymph nodes.

"HEY," SUZY SAYS, slurring chew-spit into her Coke can. "What do you call a Mexican woman with seven kids?" I try to shrug away the punchline but Sal gives his big-lipped smirk and asks what. "Consuelo," Suzy says, her mouth a snarl of glee. She puts her hand down between her knees, mimes a pendulum.

I smile in a way that I guess is not convincing because Suzy says, "What's the matter, Jerr-Bear?" I tell her the joke's not funny.

"Fuck you it isn't."

"Think I'll do my geographics."

"You do that," Suzy says, turning back to Sal. "Can't leave you here with Pockets all shift." Pockets being what Suzy calls me in her kinder moments, when she doesn't feel like "Smartass" or "Thesaurus" or "Mama's boy." Something to do with I guess I put my hands in my coverall pockets too much. I walk away while Sal starts saying something about Donaldson or Bautista and Suzy makes her usual joke about me and the Maglite.

Before she got sick, Eileen used to work in research, and on slow days, that is, most days, I used to think up towards her. I'd look at the shiny glass windows of the research build-ing and imagine Eileen working on the other side. Mostly what they do up there is ergonomic self-assessments and loss-prevention self-assessments but sometimes they do cutting and cracking. A lot of what they do is sit there staring at glove matrices and gauges and screens but I'd always pic-ture Eileen with her hands in the biosafety cabinet. I'd picture her in goggles and full facemask and fire-retardant suit, reaching through the little window to mix the catalyst in and then watching the crude react in the microscope. Because when Eileen was working she loved precision and she loved getting it right but most of all she loved watching the oil split and change and mutate. Say what you want about oil but the way Eileen described it she always made it seem beautiful: dense and thick, a million different shades of black. She used to say how the strange thing with oil is that if you trace it back far enough you see that it's life, that all this hydrocarbon used to be vegetables and minerals and zooplankton. Organisms that got caught down there in some cavern where they've been stewing for five hundred million years. How strange it is to look out at this petroleum Xanadu and think that all the unseen sludge running through it was life, once—that it was all compost, all along.

IN 2003 THERE was a blackout all across Ontario and the northeastern United States. A blackout caused by a software bug and what happened was people could see the stars again from cities. In dense urban areas the Milky Way was suddenly visible again, streaming through the unplugged vast. What also happened was babies, nine months later a horde of blackout babies, the hospitals overwhelmed with newborns because what else do you do when the power goes down. But if you lived in Sarnia what you would remember is the plants. It was nighttime when the power went out and what happened was an emergency shutdown of all systems, meaning all the tail gas burning at once. So every flare from all sixty-two refineries began shooting off together, a tail gas Disneyland shimmering through the river-limned night.

THE DAY SHIFT crawls along. QC QC QC. The highlight is a funny-sounding line we fix by increasing the backpressure. Delivery trucks roll in and out. The pigeons coo and shit and garble in their roosts in the stacks. Freighters park at the dock and pump the tanks full of bitumen—the oil moving, as always, in secret, shrouded behind cylindrical veils of carbon steel. Engineers cruise through tapping iPads, printing the readings from Suzy's board. Swarms of contractors pass by. I stick a cold water bottle in each pocket, which is nice for ten minutes then means I'm carrying piss-warm water around the unit. I do my geographic checks, walk around the tower turning the odd valve when Suzy radios, watch the river rush and kick by the great hulls of the freighters. I think about leaping onto the back of one of those freighters, letting it drag me down the St. Clair and into Erie just to feel the lick of breeze on neck.

In the Bio unit, we deal with wastewater. Like the rest of the units we heat and boil. We use hydrobonds and boilers and piston pumps. We monitor temperatures. Unlike the other units, we don't want to make oil. We want to make clean water. There are standards, degrees of toxicity. There are cuts, enzymes that we put into the water in the right doses to break down the hydrocarbons, to reduce the waste.

Time sags and sags and yawns. By 10:00 a.m. I can feel the sun howling off the concrete, rising up vengeful and gummy. Doesn't matter that it's mid-June and already there's a heat warning, you've still got to wear your cover-alls and your steel toes and your hard hat, the sweat gooing up the insides of your arms, licking the backs of your knees. The heat warning means we take "precautions." It means coolers full of Nestlé water sweating beside the board. It means we walk slowly around the unit. As slow as we can possibly move but the slow walking becomes its own challenge because the work's still got to get done.

The river gets me through the shift: the curl and cool of it, its great improbable blue. The cosmic-bright blue that's supposedly caused by the zebra mussels the government put all over Ontario to make the water blue and pretty but if Eileen were here she'd say her thing about the algae. How she learned in first-year bio that what the zebra mussels do is eat all the particles from the lake, allowing room for algae to grow beyond their boundaries and leading to massive poisonous algae blooms in Lake Huron and Lake Erie. So you think you're fixing something but really there's no fixing and how fitting that one way or another the river's livid blue is both beautiful and polluted, toxic and sublime.

THERE'S A TRAIN that runs beneath the river, from Sarnia to Port Huron and back. An industry train, bringing ethylene here and PVC there. On shift I often think of it running back and forth down there, fifty or a hundred feet below the ground where we stand and work. I picture it wending through the underground, the strange world full of the dried-up oil reservoirs, salt caverns where miners have slipped and fallen to suffocate in a great halite throat. It's hard to detect with the hydraulics and the million different vibrations but sometimes I feel or at least imagine I feel that train passing beneath me. Trundling among the groundwater and the salt and the drained chambers where peat and mud and seaweed cooked slowly for a hundred million years. Sometimes when I think of the train I think the river Styx. How Mum used to tell me about Charon the ferryman, who brought souls to the underworld. Charon travelling across the river again and again, plucking the coins from the mouths of the dead and if they couldn't pay they'd have to walk the riverbank for a hundred years. And the souls that are down there are the souls of primordial beings that died suddenly and then stewed underground for eras and epochs and finally came up gushing and were gone.

"HEARD ABOUT THOSE bodies?" Sal asks, thumbing through his phone as I pass by the board. I ask what bodies and he says the ones in Toronto. "Like a half dozen of them, some kind of landscaper-murderer stashing bodies in planters all over the city."

"Isn't that old news?"

Sal shrugs, his thumb swiping through newsfeed blue. Hard to say, sometimes, how those cycles work. "Doesn't make it less fucked up."

I kill the shift as usual: walk around wiggling the flashlight thinking about the different spots in the river and diving into them with my mind. Thinking about what might be sleeping down there—maybe a pike or a smelt or a rainbow trout nestled among the algae and the old glass Coke bottles. Sometimes I think my way across the bridge, over to Port Huron. Wonder if there's an operator over there doing the same thing, thinking back across the river towards me.

I drive home the long way which means corn fields and wind turbines in the distance as the sky steeps crimson and rose. In the thickening dark, I think of those bodies, the ones Sal was talking about. Bruce McArthur. I remember hearing about it—this killer targeting gay men in Toronto and the more planters they dug up the more bodies they found. Body parts buried among the city's carefully strategized vegetal veinwork—a jawbone in the harebell, a scatter of teeth in the bluestem, a pair of eyeballs forgotten in the bergamot. In the rear-view a flare shoots up from the plants. Getting closer, I pass through a gauntlet of turbines, feeling them more than I see them. Carbon-filament sentries. Once I passed an enormous truck carrying a wind turbine blade and at first I thought it was a whale. It reminded me of videos I'd seen of Korean authorities transporting a sperm whale bloated with methane, belching its guts across the tarmac. The truck had a convoy and a bunch of orange WIDE LOAD signs and I passed it slowly, partly because of the danger and partly because there was a pulse to it, something drawing me in. The great sleek curve of the blade, its unreal whiteness.

EILEEN'S STILL UP, vaping in her chair by the window. "Sorry," she says, spinning her chair to look at me. "Couldn't sleep." I tell her she can vape in the kitchen or wherever she likes but she looks at me with her stoned slanting smile and tells me it's not that. Says how she's been looking out into the yard a lot and when she does she thinks about the teenagers. She looks at me like she wants me to ask for details. I don't, but she continues anyway. Rehearses how those kids in the seventies got trapped in the abandoned fallout shelter. "You know, the yards were so long because the properties used to be cottages and the old shelter was overgrown and the teens were skipping school and smoking up and the excavator came through and started to fill it in and no one realized the teens were missing until days later. The only explanation was that they were scared, so scared of getting caught that they stayed quiet, let it happen, hoped it would pass."

"You don't believe all that do you?"

Eileen shrugs, still staring out the window. "No. Maybe. I just like the story."

I ask how's the pain today and she says manageable. Turns her face towards me but doesn't meet my eyes. I ask her out of ten and she says you know I hate that. She asks is something wrong, something else. I tell her no. "Seems like there's something you're not telling me about." I don't respond and she doesn't push it.

We watch the original *Total Recall* and when we get to the part with the three-breasted woman Eileen asks if I find that strange or sexy and I tell her neither, or both. Eventually Eileen drifts off but when I stand up she lurches awake. She asks where I'm going and I say just downstairs to read the new *Deadpool* unless she wants the bedside lamp on. She says no, asks when I'm coming to bed. I tell her soon and she says cuddle me when you get here. "Don't just lie there," she says. "Hold me." I tell her yes, of course, and head down to the sweet dank sogg of the basement.

Mum listens with tender quiet as I tell her about my day—about Suzy, about the pigeons, about the construction. Mum nods and smiles, gentle and sweet, her gold incisor catching light from the bare pull-string bulb. Eventually I check my phone and see that it's pushing eleven and I should probably head upstairs if I want my six to seven hours. I give Mum a good night kiss and tell her to get some rest and then I notice something strange in the floor, stoop down to inspect.

A hand-shaped imprint in the foundation.

Mum looks on, her face a void, as I toe that dark patch with my basement-blackened sock and find that it's wet, somewhat soggy. The hole's a bit sandy and when I get closer I smell it. Muskeg. Skunky Lambton crude.

I prod a little deeper and become a stranger, become someone who would stick a curious thumb into such a cavity. The oil comes out gooey and black and smelling sharp, a little sulphurous.

I DREAM OF the bodies buried in planters in Toronto. In the dream the bodies aren't skeletons, not yet. They're in the active decay stage: their organs starting to liquefy, the soft tissue browning and breaking down while the hair, teeth, and bone remain intact. I see them crawling up from planters all across the city. Not vengeful or anything. Just digging, rising, trying to get back.

"WOULD YOU HAVE liked to become an engineer?" Eileen sips her iced tea in the bug tent. Eileen's just finished her shift, run the algorithms, the computer humming in the basement searching all the contests in the world. Outside the tent the charivari of loaders and bulldozers, the air heady with the lilt of tar.

"I am one. A chemical engineer." I can see Eileen wanting to laugh and fighting it. Not like I've got any delusions about my four-year Lambton College diploma but technically it is a credential in chemical engineering.

"Maybe an urban planner," Eileen says. "Have you heard about all this stuff they're doing in cities now? Condos with elevators big enough for cars. Cute little electric cars that you'll bring right up to your apartment with you."

"Sounds more like an Eileen thing."

A bird lands in the armpit of the oak. A pocket-sized black bird with a slash of red on its wing. The one I love but can never remember its name.

Eileen sips her tea and says yeah I'm probably right but it's just she can tell the hours are getting to me. The hours and the nights and the overtime. She reminds me how I told her, once, that it's like a sickness, the overtime.

"You could do whatever you want," she says. "You could be so much."

The worst part is she always means it and the worst part is it's not true. Not true because Mum worked part-time and Dad died so young that there was no money for me to do anything but CPET. I don't tell her because she already knows about the comics store, about how maybe I could write a comic on the side and I already have the character—BioMe, the scientist turned mutant tree-man after attempting to splice photosynthesis into the human genome.

"You're so creative, you could be so much. Like your comics store idea. And remember that musical you wrote in high school, *Hydrocarbonia*?" She chuckles. "There was that three-eyed coyote and the plant worker Village People chorus?"

"I think it was basically a *Simpsons* rip-off. Mr. Hunter went with *Guys and Dolls*."

"Still. You're a poet at heart."

"The bard of bitumen."

"What I mean is I love you but sometimes I feel like all you do is work and all I do is sleep and we never see each other and I just wish we had something else, something more."

A quick haze of stupidity in which I contemplate telling her about Mum. Then I see a seagull in the distance, watch as it catches a thermal and rides high and higher, an albatross floating through the glazed crantini sky.

"One more shift," I tell her. "Then four off."

She doesn't need to roll her eyes. "Look," she says, pointing up at the oak. "A red-winged blackbird."

ON THE DRIVE to work they're saying about the fish. Saying about the drinking water downstream, in Windsor and Michigan. Saying about the tritium spilling into Lake Huron. You think Chernobyl and you think Blinky the Three-Eyed Fish but what you don't think is an hour north or so, where Bruce Power leaks barrels of radioactive tritium into Lake Huron. They're saying how significant quantities of antidepressants have been found in fish brains in the Great Lakes.

I drive past the rusting drums and have to stop for a moment because there are some protesters forming a drum circle. They're holding signs that read STOP LINE 9 and chanting about stolen land and of course they're right but I don't smile or stop or acknowledge them. Just park and walk through security, a new sting in the awful. At the gates the bent-toothed security guard is sitting in his white SUV next to the NO TRESPASSING sign. The guard waves, tweaks his wraparounds, the river glowing purple in his mirrored lenses.

WAYS PEOPLE DEAL with constant low-level dread: the myth that the wind blows the fumes south, towards Aamjiwnaang, towards Corunna, towards Walpole. That the airborne toxicity lands ten kilometres to the south. That the people who live north of the plants won't get sick or at least not as sick. As if wind could really dilute the impact of living beside a cluster of sixty-two petrochemical refineries that never sleep, could change the fact that you live in a city where Pearl Harbor–style sirens sound their test alarm every Monday at 12:30 to remind you that leaks could happen at any moment. There's a joke around Streamline, a joke that is not a joke: the retirement package is great if you make it to fifty-five. Which is not inaccurate in my family seeing as Dad went at fifty-two and Mum followed at fifty-six and they said the lung cancer had nothing to do with the plants and the brain cancer had nothing to do with Mum's daily swims from the bridge to Canatara Beach. The strange pride among people who work the plants: spending-your-oil-salary-on-Hummers-and-motorcycles-and-vacations-to-Cuban-beaches-with-plastic-cups kind of pride. A live-rich, live-hard kind of pride. The yippee ki yay of knowing that Sarnia is the leukemia capital of Canada and the brain cancer capital of Canada and the air pollution capital of Canada but also knowing that oil is what you know and what your parents knew and all your family's in Lambton County so what else are you going to do but stay.

WE'RE PUTTING ON our facemasks and backpacks while Don the safety protocol officer explains for the hundredth time about the new model of self-contained breathing apparatus and the new standard-issue Kevlar gloves. Telling us once again that personal safety is paramount even though all of us know that what operators are here for is to control situations.

I'm sitting there watching sailboats tack their way across the lake while Don goes on about the hydrogen sulfide incident that happened two years ago. Incident meaning leak. Telling us again how the thing about hydrogen sulfide is that you can't see it, so there's almost no way of knowing when it's on fire. Two years ago when a vehicle melted in the loading dock an invisible sulfide fire came through and before the operators could shut it down the truck in the loading bay just melted. The tires evaporated and the air hissed out of them and the whole truck sank to the floor, a puddle of melted paint on the concrete and nothing left of the truck but a gleaming skeleton of carbon steel.

WE USED TO swim in the lake at night, just the two of us. Dad was usually home watching the Blue Jays so me and Mum would drive up to a secret little beach in the north and we'd swim out into the middle of the river where the lights from Port Huron gleamed and wiggled in the darkness. Sometimes it would rain and the rain would make the water warmer than the air. I'd seen a water snake at the beach once and I always imagined them down there among our legs. Though Mum had assured me they were nonvenomous, I saw them sharp-toothed and cunning, biding their time. Sometimes Mum would dip down below the water, her head disappearing for what seemed an impossibly long time and I don't know how she found me but she'd wrangle her arms around both my legs and pin me for a moment while I kicked and bucked and then we'd both come up gasping and squealing and giggling in the black water, a gelatin dazzle of refinery lights.

"SO WHAT TREE?" Eileen asks, watching the sun bleed pink delirium over the abandoned Libcor refinery. Eileen in her chair and the van parked behind us. In front, the overgrown refinery that shut down thirty years ago after a mercaptan leak. When they left, the company kept the lot. Took down all the tall buildings and left a waste of concrete with a railway running through it, surrounded by a barbed-wire fence.

I ask for clarification and Eileen asks what tree I'd want to be buried in and I pause to think about it, looking out over the crabgrass and sumac and firepits full of scorched goldenrod. "Think there are any animals in there?"

Eileen says yeah, probably, like Chernobyl. She knows about Chernobyl from a documentary. In the Exclusion Zone, there's a place called the Red Forest. It's a bit stunted and the trees have a strange ginger hue but the wildlife is thriving—boar, deer, wolves, eagles. Eileen says how nuclear radiation might actually be better for animals than human habitation.

I stand quietly, holding Eileen's chair and watching the sun pulse and glow and vanish. She reaches back and takes my hand, rubs the valleys between my fingers. Eventually, without saying anything, we turn for the van.

"You ever think about concrete?" Eileen asks as I'm fastening her chair into the van. "How it seems so permanent. How it's all around us and we walk and drive on it believing it's hard and firm and solid as the liquid rock it is but really it's nothing like rock at all. Weeds and soil beneath it and all of it ready to rise up at the gentlest invitation. It's very fragile, very temporary."

On the way home we pass by the rubber plant and the abandoned Bluewater Village and beyond it Aamjiwnaang and Eileen says, "Incredible shrinking territory." The reserve used to stretch from Detroit to the Bruce Peninsula before being slowly whittled down through centuries of sketchy land deals. Eileen's maternal grandmother was Ojibwe and she has three cousins on the reserve and we go over once in a while but mostly her tradition is just to say "incredible shrinking territory" when we drive by.

It comes to me when we pass a bungalow, spot a clutch of them crawling up from the cleft of the foundation. "Sumac, I guess."

"What?"

I say sumac again and Eileen clues in and says aren't those basically weeds? I tell her no, they can get pretty big and I like the fruit, how they go red in autumn. I like how they're sort of bushy and don't have a prominent trunk. How they're spunky and fierce and unpredictable.

"Sumac." Eileen does her pondering frown. "Noted."

It's dark now and the lights are on in Port Huron, flickering out over the river. Looking out the window, Eileen asks me to tell her again how the county used to be. I hold on to the wheel and steer through the great chandelier and tell it how Mum used to. I say about the plank road and the Iroquois Hotel, how Petrolia was incorporated the very year Canada became a country, so we're basically built on oil. I tell about the gushers in every field, soaring up fifty feet and raining down on the fields, clogging up the river and the lakes until the fishermen in Lake Erie complained about the black grit on the hulls of their boats. I tell about the notorious stench of the Lambton skunk, and about the fires. No railway or fire trucks and so when lightning hit and fire took to the fields they often burned for weeks at a time, a carnage of oil fire raging through the night.

"Wild," she says. "Can you believe all that's gone now? That whole world."

I don't say it's not gone, just invisible—racing through stacks and columns and broilers. I tell her what a perfect word: "wild."

EILEEN GOES TO bed early so I head down to the damp lull of the basement. The hole is the size of a Frisbee now, and it's starting to stink. I sit on the old plastic-plaid lawn chair and talk to Mum about work, about Suzy, about the fish and the pigeons and the ratio.

There's a long silence. I didn't know the whole thing was getting to me. Didn't know how it was building in me, fierce and rank. I tell Mum I'm worried. Worried I'm going to lose her. Worried about the smell, the secrets. Worried someone's going to figure it out, maybe talk to Virgil the taxidermist. And I can't tell Eileen and the whole thing is sorry, rotten, and what are we going to do, what am I going to do?

Mum sits there and listens sweetly. Then she twinkles her golden incisor towards the muskeg hole and I see something strange, something wrong, something white. So I step closer, grab an old chair leg and stir the muskeg a little and yes it definitely is what I think it is: a small bone that could easily be a piece of a raccoon thigh but could also be a human finger.

I WAKE UP at 5:00 p.m. and find Eileen making pesto, which means a good day. She's got the contest software going on the table. "Six wins already!" she says as I'm making a Keurig. "Want to go to South Carolina? There's these subway cars. Fake coral reefs. Vina and Phil are planning a trip."

I pour milk into my Ninja Turtles mug and she tells me there's another one in the toilet. "Sorry." She winces, pouring olive oil on a mound of basil and parm. "I wanted to. Just didn't have the energy." She presses a button on the KitchenAid, makes whirling mayhem of leaf and oil.

I put on my spare Kevlars and head into the bathroom, pull the lid up to find the rat floundering, scrambling, its teeth bared and wet with fresh blood from where it must have bludgeoned itself against the porcelain. The water the colour of rust. The rat keeps trying to run up the side of the toilet, losing its purchase and sliding back down in a carnage of thrashing legs and sploshing water.

Without quite knowing why, I reach in and pin the rat and squat down to look into its eyes. I guess I want to know what it's like to be a rat. Its head flicks back and forth in rage or terror, never meeting my eyes. Maybe it doesn't know how to.

If I let it go it'll just end up back here, in the toilet, in pain. So I hold its head under the water. Pin it as it thrashes and bucks and wheels its legs, switching its ghost-pink tail. Exhausted, the creature doesn't fight much. More or less lets it happen.

I walk it through a Stonehenge of pylons and descend into the guts of the exhumed city street. I lay the rat in a puddle at the mouth of a culvert and throw some sludge over it. Walk back between a mound of PVC piping and a wrecked Jenga of blasted asphalt.

Back inside, I tell Eileen I released it alive. "Good," she says. "I'm getting tired of this. Must have something to do with the plumbing, the construction."

"Should be over soon."

"What should?"

"Want to go down to the river?"

We park at Point Edward and I wheel Eileen down to the waterfront, where the river curls and snarls and chops its dazzling blue. Underfoot there's a belligerence of goose shit. We watch a pair and Eileen tells me they mate for life and get fierce about their young. They've been known to attack adult humans to protect them. I look at the geese and wonder how long their families have been nesting on this river.

"When did they stop migrating?" Eileen asks.

Which makes me think of a book I read once, where the main character keeps asking where the ducks go in winter. I can't remember what book or what the answer was, if there was one. I tell her I don't know and she tells me how weird it is that there's this whole big thing about Canada geese flying south in winter but as far as she can tell they never leave.

"I think it's the northern ones, more so."

"And what, they migrate down here? Winter in scenic Sarnia?"

Beneath the bridge a teenager launches into a backflip. Executes perfectly to uproarious applause. His audience: a chubby red-headed boy and three thin girls in dripping bathing suits. Eileen stops for a moment and I can see her watching them and maybe she's thinking how comfortable they are. How cozy. How nice it must be to just have a body and not think about it.

Above them, transport trucks arc through a highway in the sky.

THE FOUR OFF blurs by in a haze of Domino's and Netflix and assuring Eileen there's no smell from the basement, that it's probably just the construction. Eileen and I watch all of *Jessica Jones*, then all of *The Punisher*, listen to the bleats and chirps of loaders and excavators. On Saturday I find a bone like a human elbow joint in the muskeg, another like an eye socket. Rodent hip, I convince myself. Racoon brow. Squirrel bits. More rats.

Then it's Sunday, meaning back to night shift for eight more on. I'm whizzing past corn fields on the way to work when I notice something strange, something I've never spotted. Which makes sense because it's in the very back of the field and it sort of blends in with a little patch of windbreak trees behind it but there it is: a rusted old derrick in the middle of the corn field. An iron steeple rising up through the swishing haze like a puncture in time, a throwback to the days of gushers and teamsters, when the fields were choked with oil and fires burned for weeks.

Eileen texts me to say there's still that weird smell in the house and she's pretty sure it's oil or gas. Maybe it's the stove, should she be worried? She's thinking of texting her brother to come check it out. I tell her no, don't text your brother, I'll open the windows when I get home. Which is when I hear the enunciator.

The blare of the Class A and then the radio crunches and Suzy comes on saying there's a few malfunction lights on in Zone 1 and a flare shooting off. "Main concern is FAL-250A. Flow transfer failure could be a big one, let's get on it."

When a Class A sounds, everyone goes. So it's not just us Bio unit operators scurrying around, it's also CDU and Naphtha and Alkylation and Plastics and the unit is full of bodies. Doug puts on an SCBA though nobody's sure why. Derek and Paul smash into each other at full speed on the Tower 1 scaffold causing Suzy to yell, "No-fucking-running rule still fucking holds." Stan, one of the night engineers, says maybe it could have something to do with the sludge blanket level in the wastewater valve.

Suzy wheels on him. "How the fuck is that?" When Stan starts to explain she tells him to go back to his craft beer and his Magic card tournaments.

Jack tries again: "Backpressure?"

Suzy glares at him, leaking chew-spit onto the floor. Stan walks off muttering something about valve monkeys. Suzy stares at her board and calls orders out while the rest of us scramble around checking valves and lines and readings.

Sal finds the problem: a release valve is down and there's buildup in the main flare. A buildup of hydrocarbon waste in the thirty-six-inch flare where the tail gas should be burning off, which means a lot of flammable gunk and Suzy's board is telling her the flare's going but the flare is not going.

"Looks like a problem with the pilot flame," Sal shouts from halfway up the tower.

"Getting enough oxygen?" Stan shouts back up.

"Should probably call research," Sal says. Suzy says fuck those fucking lab monkeys then moves towards the tower with a gunslinger strut. Grabbing a rag from a maintenance cart, she starts tying it around a plunger. She sets a boot down on the rubber cup and yanks the wooden handle free. Then she climbs up the tower to the first platform. As she's heading up Sal races down and I'm backing off too as Suzy leans back, shouts, "Heads up," and sends the plunger handle arcing towards the mouth of the flare.

The workers scatter—scurrying into the warehouse and the delivery building, hunching behind trucks and the board. I find a dumpster and cling to the back of it. Sal hits the concrete and joins me just in time to watch the plunger arc and arc and land in the maw of the stack.

The air shimmies and buckles.

The flare lights.

Lights and blasts seventy feet into the moon-limned sky. Air swirls and booms and I clutch my chest because I can't breathe.

The dumpster jumps.

The dumpster becomes a toad and leaps ten feet across the floor. The flare lights, a hissing rage of tail gas, a seventy-foot Roman candle stabbing up at the sickle moon.

No one gets hurt. No one gets in trouble. Stan walks away shaking his head along with the ten or twelve operators gathered on the floor. The enunciator goes quiet and Suzy walks down from the stack brushing off her knees.

Sal looks over at me, muttering something about being too old for these shenanigans. He walks away huffing, pauses to curse towards the dumpster's skid mark, which is longer than a car. Suzy calls me over and tells me I didn't see shit, then tells me to look after the flare for the rest of my shift.

"What do you mean 'look after it'?"

"Stand there and watch it, Stephen fucking Hawking."

So I stand there and watch it.

The moon grins down and the flame shoots up beside it for ten minutes, then twenty, with no sign of abating. I pace around Tower 1, checking pressures and temps and turning valves as needed but always keeping that flare in eyeshot.

One hour. Two.

Down by the river I see the lakeshore going liquid and sort of throbbing. At first I think it must be gas. Then I think I must be hallucinating because the shoreline itself has turned semi-solid as it refracts the flare's corona. It looks like there's flesh down there, a great beast sidling up to the fence.

I walk down and shine my flashlight on the shore and see that it is flesh. Not one creature, but thousands. Smelt. Thousands and thousands of smelt cozying up to the shore, coming as close as they can to the flame.

I don't notice Suzy until she's gusting sour breath over my shoulder. "The fuck is that?"

"Smelt."

She stands there looking at the fish awhile, spitting into her Coke can. Then she turns back to her flare, gives it the up-down. For a moment I think she might genuflect.

"Fucking smelt," she scoffs, walking away.

I spend the rest of the shift watching the smelt shudder in the balm of the flare. Thousands of fish inching towards the tail gas column as it roars and rages through the punctured dark. Light licking them silver and bronze, the smelt push and push against the shore—close and closer but never close enough.

I DRIVE HOME past the wind turbines thinking as I often do about a hundred thousand years from now when maybe someone would come across this place. I talked about this once, with Mum. We walked into a corn field just to look at the turbines and when we got there I asked what would happen if there were no corn or soy or farmers left, just the turbines marking the graves of fields. How maybe a thousand years from now there would be a new kind of people like in *Mad Max* and they wouldn't remember farms or electricity or the nuclear power plant in Kincardine. How these future humans might find this place where turbines sprouted up taller than any trees, their arms like great white whales. The surrounding farms all gone to wild again. And what else would these new people think but that these massive three-armed hangmen were slow-spinning gods? "That's very well put," Mum said then, as if she were the teacher she'd always wanted to be instead of being a woman who answered the phones at NRCore three days a week. She stood beneath that turbine, staring up at its bland white belly for a long time before she finally said, "It does sort of look like a god. A faceless god."

Eileen's still sleeping when I get home so I pour some Merlot and head straight down through the oil reek into the basement. Eileen was right. The smell is getting bad. Detectable from the kitchen and almost unbearable in the basement itself and what this means is a matter of days at most. The morning sun winks and flickers through the cracked foundation. The hole is the size of a truck tire now and there are more bones floating at the surface. I grab an old broken chair leg and stir the muck around, transfixed by the bones. One that looks like a splintered T-bone, one that may be a gnawed jawbone, another that I'm pretty sure has part of a fingernail attached. A row of molars like a hardened stitch of corn.

The teenagers. In the yard. The story I've never believed.

"It's all right," Mum would say if she could speak. "It's all right, sweet sonny boy. You're all right, you're here, everything's going to be fine."

And Mum would be right. For the moment everything is nice and cool and dark and we sit there in the gentle silence until Mum wants me to tell her some of the old stories so I do. I tell them the way she used to tell me. I tell about her grandfather, the Lambton oil man who sniffed for gushers and got ripped off on the patent for the Canada rig. I tell about the last gusher and the time lightning struck the still and all the dirty land sales the companies made to get things started in Sarnia. Water, I remember her saying once. It was all about water. They chose Sarnia because they needed to be by the river. I tell her the same now and she sits there smiling faintly, a twinkle in her gold incisor and for the moment the two of us are calm and happy and together.

WHEN I CREEP into bed Eileen wakes up. She reaches for her bedside table, produces a rectangular LED blear. "It's almost noon," she says. "What were you doing?" I tell her I was in the basement. She asks if I was playing WoW again and I say no just reading some old volumes of *Turok*. She murmurs the usual: just don't take up Magic like her brother. I laugh and tell her no, of course not.

Then she rises. Sits up in bed and I can see even with the blackout blinds that she's gone serious. She asks if there's something going on with me lately. I tell her no, of course not, just a hard day at work. And how could you expect what comes next:

"You know I'm never going to get better?"

In these moments I can never find the right thing to say because there is no right thing.

"It's just," she continues, "sometimes I forget, myself, that it's not ever going to end, that it's just going to keep going like this for who knows how long. And I just want to be sure that you know the full extent of that."

I tell her yeah, of course.

She squints through the dark. "It's just, I know it's hard for you, and if you ever wanted—"

I tell her no, absolutely not, whatever it is. Whisper that I don't want anything different, don't need anything more than what we have. I go big spoon and nestle into her until I'm hot, until I'm roasting under the blankets and wanting to roll away but also wanting just to melt, to seep, to burn hot as compost in nitrogen night.

I DREAM BLACK water, a paddle, a smell, a funk, in front of me Mum standing, holding a punting pole. I can't see her face but I see the reflection of her gold tooth in the thick black morass, a tooth like a sun. She is gone, she remains, I am trying to call her but this is the dream's mute torture and the water is not water but sludge and in the mire there are faces, hands and faces dripping black and reaching up, grasping the pole, each other, the hull. Hands and limbs slick in the gunk the forgotten-vegetable slurry Mum leaning on the punting pole my mouth opening and straining, willing, wailing.

THE DAY DAD DIED, Mum and I sat in the bug tent in the backyard watching a horde of blue jays eat the heads off Mum's sunflowers. Any other day she would have got up and screamed carnage at those birds but she just sat there watching. He'd weighed about forty-five pounds at the end and it was not a nice thing for a wife or a fifteen-year-old son to watch. It ended graciously, in sleep. The ambulance came and Mum went with because there were checks to be done, forms to be signed. After she came home we sat in the backyard watching those ravenous blue jays pick through a row of twenty or thirty six-foot sunflowers. I said how I didn't know blue jays could be so vicious and Mum said oh yeah, everything beautiful has a dark side, just like everything wretched has a loveliness. When there were only three heads remaining and the blue jays were pecking tiredly, half of them gone, Mum told me those sunflowers had been growing in the spot where she'd buried her placenta after I was born. She said she'd always figured that's why they grew so well there. Said how the placenta had enriched the soil and so in a way I was feeding those blue jays, we both were. And so the two of us sat there watching the birds gobble up the vegetation we'd nourished together and I saw each one grow a face. The last three sunflowers became me and Dad and Mum and I watched the blue jays shred those yellow faces into mangled tufts.

I TAKE THE long way to work and when I see the wind turbines I find myself driving towards them. Driving down a farm road and then onto a corn farm with a turbine on a strip of grass and weed and I'm leaping out of the car and sprinting up to it, kneeling while this terrible white demiurge churns its arms in slow rotation. I kneel there thinking up towards that turbine and feeling overpowered by something blunt and terrible and awesome. The sound of the thing is huge and steady and sonorous, an Olympian didgeridoo, and I remember about the bats. How this strange hum draws them in and then the arms send them plummeting into the fields where the farmers have to burn them so they don't attract pests. The arms spin slow but in their slowness there's something massive, something enormous and indifferent and nearly perfect. I imagine myself chopped into atoms, into confetti. I see tiny particles of my hair and skin feathering over the field, blending with the earth and the soil, becoming vegetable, becoming corn. The wholeness of that resignation, a longing to be unmade, to wilt beyond worry and debt, pension and disease.

The farmer whizzes over on an ATV. Behind the quad there's a trailer carrying a blue chemical drum, the skull-and-crossbones symbol on the side. The farmer asks if I'm all right and I tell him sure, fine, never better.

"Well then," he says.

I walk away wondering how much ethanol's in the soil.

THE NIGHT SHIFT sags and sputters. Clouds brood and curdle over the river. I get a text from Eileen saying she's smelling that oil smell again and is she going insane? I text back not to worry, it's just the construction, I'll phone the city tomorrow. I tell myself don't check the phone don't check the phone and then I check and it says that Eileen's brother's on the way.

What I do is panic. What I do is leave, which is a fireable offence. What I do is vacate my coveralls there in the middle of the unit with Suzy walking through shouting don't even think about it but I need to get home and so I just say, "Be right back," and hustle to my car without showering.

What I do is drive tilting and teetering and when I get home Eileen's brother's truck is in the driveway among the shadowy hulks of graders and loaders lurking against the orange plastic mesh. Eileen's in her chair at the top of the stairs saying sorry, she had to, the smell, and then her brother saw what was downstairs. She looks at me, a little broken.

"I'm sorry."

"It's okay. It's weird, super-weird. It's fucked, Jerr. But we can deal with it. We can talk about it. You're hurting, you're troubled." She reaches out and I sink my hand in hers, let her squeeze it.

I head down into the basement where Eileen's brother, Gord, stands in street clothes over the muskeg pit, his back to Mum. They've moved her slightly, pulled her beneath the stark light of the pull-string bulb. Up close, she looks bad. Wrinkly and purplish, with a sickly glaze.

I reach out to embrace her and Gord says no, don't, not a good idea. I ask him am I under arrest and he talks to the floor. Says he's sorry, he should be taking me downtown already but he's doing Eileen a favour. I'm lucky he's in street clothes but he's still a cop. He sucks his teeth, looks at me a little pale, struggling to meet my eyes. "This is a serious fucking bind, Jerr."

I nod to Mum: "What'll happen to her?"

He winces. "We'll have to confiscate the body. Evidence."

I step closer and hug Mum tight, press my face against hers and kiss both cheeks. Pull away and look deep into her face, which has been in the shadows but is visible now, a snaggle of resin and vein.

My pocket beeps. A text from Suzy: *The fuck are you? Get back here emergency all hands.* I don't consult Gord, just turn and head for the steps. His voice barking behind me, talking about coroners, about extenuating circumstances and covering his ass. Gord shouting station sooner or later but I'm gone, rising, out of the basement.

THE ENUNCIATOR'S GOING Class A and everyone's running around frantic as I scramble into my coveralls and grab an SCBA and head out to Tower 1. Sal's walking away from the scene, heading for the parking lot. "Fuck this," he grumbles into his SCBA helmet. "Not worth it."

I ignore him, keep going, suddenly beyond worry, over fear. When I look up I can see a red alert light blinking by the broiler on Tower 1, so I head over and climb the stairs.

Suzy's down below and shouting, "Back inside back inside," but she can't be talking to me because I'm floating. Floating very slowly, the world turned heavy and blurry. There's a strange heat and a haze in the air and Suzy's shouting, "Inside inside," but now I'm starting to think she might be shouting, "Sulfide," is clearly shouting, "Sulfide." Which seems funny. Which seems hilarious. Which seems perfect.

The enunciator ratchets up a notch.

Below, the hydrants swivel their R2-D2 heads and let loose. Twenty hydrants sending millions of gallons of water arcing through the air to knock the gas off and that, too, is hilarious.

In the distance, turbines churn and churn and churn like children's pinwheels, blowing all the bad air far far away.

I keep climbing. The hydrants arc and spit and soak me. I slip on the latticed steel stairs and recover and get to the valve near the alert light, start to turn it but it's heavy, wildly heavy. Comically heavy as I lean in and stagger a little and then get it turning, get it shut.

On the way back to the stairs my legs are bendy like bubble gum. I take a step and then wilt into a kind of human puddle. Writhing onto my stomach, I see through the platform's steel grid two ambulances and a fire truck raging into the parking lot. My SCBA's bleating like a duck or a bulldozer and in the distance there are sirens, beautiful sirens. The hydrants spit their applause, twenty tearful arcs of triumph.

Eileen appears beside me, flapping turbine arms. I move to speak her name but she shushes me, fern-teeth wavering in the bog of her mouth. Her tongue is a hundred sea-snakes and she's saying shush, never mind, she's come to take me away. As I'm clutching the nubs on her scaly green withers, I ask what happened to Mum, to the basement muskeg. She tells me diverted pipeline and the company will pay us off and Mum's all right now, it's time to let her go. And of course she's right, Eileen. Of course she's always been perfect and right and brave, so brave.

She starts to flap her turbine wings and soon we're chugging up and soaring, cruising, swooping high over the river, the hydrants swirling through the sky below. Eileen curls into a loop-de-loop and when we come back up I can see that the hydrants have become gushers. Twenty black fountains arcing and curling through the floodlit night. Down below, a million neon-blue smelt dance calypso at the surface of the river. Mum stands beneath the bridge, looking up and waving, her face no longer discoloured, her gold incisor gleaming.

I glance over at Eileen, her green eyes glowing elfin and wild. I tell her I have something to confess and she says she knows, she always knew. She says it's a little weird, the thing with me and Mum, but what isn't a little weird?

We catch hold of a thermal that takes us up fast, too fast, high above the black arcs of the fountains. The air strobes and changes colour and Eileen twirls a wing and says, "Look." What I see is a sky full of plants. Coral and krill and strange ancient grasses and we're riding it, soaring on the spirits of five hundred million years and for once it is not bad, is not sickening. All around us the gleaming ghosts of sedge and bulrushes, zooplankton and anemones and all of it pulsing green again. Below the river full of dancing neon smelt as Eileen spreads her wings and jags her beak and tells me it was true, was always true: we were all compost, all along. I tell her thank you and I love you, cling to her wings as we rise up burning through the broken brilliant sky.

LEVIATHAN

HE WOKE TO the shush of the door, jamb grinding snow, the sudden cold working through him. Ragged remnant of a dream—a woman with a punting pole, lank hair, a slash of gold tooth. To the east the sun rose pale and pink among the stained fields cluttered with stumps and carts and three-pole derricks. In the doorway Lise sucked her hand into her gut, hunched against the cold. The three-month pout of her, dark pools of her eyes. She shivered and stooped, waved him inside. Around him the snow was pocked with spirals of his footsteps. He raised his bare left foot, the raw weight of it like a foreign thing. His toes marbled violet and white. He remembered his father, his stubborn father still out in Wyoming or worse.

"Again?" she said. "How long've you been out here?"

"Don't know."

"Come in," she hissed, pulling her nightshirt around her stomach. She led him up the stoop, onto the stool in front of the hearth, his feet dragging melt across the floor. He danced foot to foot and thought of his father dozing in the Whole Hog or sleeping curled into a sheep or deciding he'd brave the road home in the storm. Malcolm had begged the old man to stay overnight in Wyoming and his father'd chuckled quietly, folding cheesecloth over oatcake.

Lise climbed up to the loft and pitched the bearskin over the edge, came down and saw him setting it over his feet. "No," she said. "Lie on it." She dragged the armchair over and set his feet on it. "Higher than the heart," she said.

He looked at his toes, black around the nails, purplish grey closer to the knuckles. He took the iron and sat wincing and biting as he pushed the coals. She filled the kettle and hung it on the hearth, set another pot of water on the coals, laid a hiss of embers on the lid. Heat licked out into the room as cinders rose and swirled. In the corner leered the crude crib his father had made for them as a wedding gift five years before.

The sharp heat worked through the base of his toes and into the pads of his feet and he thought how strange that cold should burn. She took the kettle from the hearth and poured him water. He sipped it and felt the freeze turning pain as if an egg was breaking inside him. She knelt beside him, reaching in and rubbing her palms on the bottoms of his feet. "Wiggle your toes." He did so and found Lise smiling, showing her brown middle tooth. Stroking his temple with the back of her hand, whispering, "Good."

She went up to sleep and he lay thirsty and weak. No point worrying now, there'd be no word or there would. He'd be fine or he wouldn't. He tried to climb up to the loft but could not for his toes. Snow glowed in the window, an oil fire burning on a distant field. He hobbled back to the armchair and poked at the fire, thinking of the swell of her in the loft. Two months before she had woken him and said she had that good feeling back. He knelt and blew into the coals, watched them pulse, shadows shifting on the lintel.

He heard the footsteps before the knock. Swung the door open to find the postmaster, Hitchens, saying they'd found his father's horse. Hitchens shivered in the doorway, a rose of frostnip on his nose. Malcolm thought down to the blackened toes inside his socks. Reaching inside his socks, he found a horde of numb blisters. Hitchens shuffled inside, stood on the sheepskin knocking one boot off the other, huffing into his hands.

"Just the horse?"

The postmaster swallowed. "Dead." Hitchens combed ice out of his red beard. "Frozen solid," he said. "Bled open."

Malcolm heard Lise stir in the loft. "Tracks?"

"None to follow." Hitchens shrugged. "A mess of them. Panic."

"You going?" Lise called.

"How far?" he asked Hitchens.

"Five miles."

A draft blew through the smoke-soiled curtain that marked his father's makeshift bedroom from the kitchen. "You'll need to eat," Lise groaned, heaving herself down the ladder.

Hitchens said he'd meet them after a couple more calls, rubbed his hands and left. Lise stood at the bottom of the ladder in her shift, hugging herself for warmth. He reached out and touched her stomach, palmed it. "You sure?" She stared back. Rocked from foot to foot on the carpet. She said nothing, far more than enough.

He went to the privy and came back to find her in her overcoat and duffle boots, holding a stick of butter and the end of yesterday's loaf. "You'll need to eat," she said again. He shrugged and hitched his boots on. The door thumped shut and she was padding up behind him into the bite of morning chill.

Sable snorted and reared but Lise clucked her calm, rubbed her withers. The horse nickered and shook a thick mist from her nostrils. Lise settled her, got the blanket and saddle on. She climbed up and raised Malcolm scrambling behind her. They turned onto Main Street, trotted past the log homes and the shanties and the red-brick bank. On the fringe of town stood the derricks in their strange elegance, snow whirling around their feet. The moon was high and clear—a half foot of fresh snow over the crust.

They left the log houses and the haste-built hotels, crossed the fields careful of the black mouths that dropped a hundred feet. They passed Malcolm's employer, the leaning storehouse. An oil fire smouldered in the south find, a few drillers with rags around their faces shovelled snow onto the blaze.

They entered the woods slow, cautious on the pocked and crusted trail. Above them stooped snow-crowned limbs. Malcolm kept hissing to go faster but Lise told him to calm himself, handed him the bread and butter. They drove north through the woods, the horse's warmth rising through them. They hit the corduroy road and passed it. The horse trotted calm through elms, willows, black ash, the beaver meadow, the broad glazed swamp.

They'd been here a decade, he and his father, had seen the derricks rise up and the speculators come off the train in gaiters and denim trousers. They'd watched the earth shudder and gush, had seen the trampled blue clay and the new plank roads. The black ash hewn and turned upside down to make the derricks. In winter the men skating on the creek next to barrels of flaming kerosene. They'd heard the geologists speaking of the unseen chasms underfoot—shale and limestone, water and gas, seas of oil.

He clung to Lise, the bounce of her thin ribs and the pouch beneath them. The sun burned through the morning haze and they trotted on until the horse stopped fast.

Blood on the snow in reckless plenty. Pocks and lumps and valleys where it had frozen over the rutted trail. On the fringe his father's chestnut curled fetal, hind legs tucked in, the left one snapped at the hock. Her throat had been slit and there was a seam cut up her barrel, the edges scummed with frozen blood and flesh.

Sable blew her nostrils, head rising through the fog. Looking at the stained snow Malcolm thought of the horse's heart, the size of it. An organ that could pump such a quantity, send it pulsing through that great brown body.

He chucked his legs down, stumbled, frostbitten toes still numb, knee buckling in the crust. He cursed and paced around the horse kicking snow and shouting for his father, screaming into the woods. A breeze passed through the hemlock, set saplings gently shivering, sloughing a dust of twinkling snow.

When he turned back to Lise he saw her pointing to his boot. A head-sized hole in the crust and as he kicked the snow loose he saw that he had sunk his heel in a slush of frozen viscera. Horse entrails. The long fat squirm of the intestine, a brittle slab of lung. His father's boots lay askew where he'd kicked them off. Malcolm leaned over to retch and coming up saw her pointing at the frozen gash along the creature's midsection.

He stepped forward, knelt, and put his palm on the horse's stomach, felt nothing but mute, cold. A frozen scar. A wound the length of a man.

He took the bowie from his belt and dug it hard into the seam, chiselled shards of ice and flesh. In a half dream he saw through the horse's barrel to the man inside. Saw the sturdy bulk of his father curled up like a baby. Saw the red-bearded man at peace, there in the horse's guts. Resting, easing, eyes blinking, quivering, finally closed.

The woods crunched with the sound of horses. Hitchens appeared with Armbruster and two Chippewa teamsters. All of them knelt, looking. The two men traded glances.

"Crawled inside?"

"Wasn't thinking straight," Lise said.

"Must've thought the warmth would keep him alive."

The teamsters produced chisels and blades, helped Malcolm hack bits from the frigid corpse until Malcolm held up a hand. "Only one way," he said with a hard look at Hitchens. The postmaster set off for benzene and the Methodist. The teamsters offered some lighting oil. They set some sacking over the heap and stood staring at the frozen horse and the white woods and the day coming on anemic over the fields.

The Methodist arrived, took Malcolm's hand and asked the age of his father. Malcolm told him and one of the teamsters lit his pipe and handed Malcolm his matches. "The Lord is merciful," the Methodist said, then turned to his book and read from the Old Testament. "'Now the days of David drew nigh…'" Lise tamped her feet in the snow, made a nervous sound in her nose. Malcolm took a step back and stared into the long scar, Brailled with hoar at the edges. "'And he charged Solomon his son, saying…I go the way of all the earth.'" Malcolm put his palm on that frost-rimmed wound, felt the cold sting of it and thought inwards, towards his father, the world spilling, tilting into the knowledge that to lose your maker is to be in some true sense unmade.

SOMEWHERE IN THE MURK of his mind there is a woman kneeling in muck, her hand at her scalp, tugging a clump of hair. A woman cradling a grey and silent thing, a wisp of hair caked red, its skin flaky, the texture of dry cheese. A woman with a red rage of hair and sixteen freckles down her back in the shape of the little dipper and she is kneeling in a spittle of rain, her shift dank with splashed mud. A woman laying the still child down in the hole at the foot of the rail-way-foraged bedrock slate into which she has scratched letters with knitting needles. He can see her muttering about her blood, the curse in it, about the one runt child she'd managed and six more, all still. Laying the child in its trench and setting a handkerchief over her fingers then reaching into her own mouth. Reaching for the one remaining incisor and commencing to pull. Rocking and humming as she prods and tugs and wags the tooth free. Stroking the cold brow of the child who never bled or breathed but whom she will remember as pain and bloat and rhythm—the thudding of limb and palm, of a turning hip, a world without breath or sight or language but no less a world.

HAVING FINISHED, THE Methodist invited Malcolm to speak before the flames. "He was a good father," Malcolm said, shivering as he tossed the match into a pool of crude at the horse's mane. "Could be a hot man. Got angry sometimes, but his love was firm—a love like a fist." Malcolm look at the cast-down eyes, the horse in the snow, the bulge of its gut. "Them's my sentiments."

Lise squeezed Malcolm's hand as the fire took. Timid, at first, the flames grew around the animal. He thought of the gut-strung banjo his father'd been given by a Virginia man he'd met on a whale ship and which he'd never learned to play but held many nights, staring into it, drumming his stained fingers on the snare. He thought of his overgrown toenails, their terrible thickness, yellow and white. He saw his father in the summer, face smudged with muskeg to ward off the mosquitoes, sawing the joints for the corners of their slapdash home, a thunderstorm gathering in the distance and his father looking up, muck-faced, unflinching, saying they'd sleep in the throat of the wind if they had to. He thought of the old man flailing up the frozen creek with crude blades tied to his boots, blazing barrels of kerosene sludge on the creekside and his father flailing useless, half drunk, his weight tossing and chucking and never quite falling, somehow holding on. He thought of the man's snore steady beneath them and as he and Lise covered each other's mouths and leaned into the straw. He thought of the glass jar of teeth his father had kept at his bedside. The teeth Malcolm's mother had pulled from her own head, one for each baby she'd lost. The time he'd pulled back the curtain and found his father sobbing silently, chest heaving, the teeth laid out in his open palm. Or the times he heard his father lay those teeth gently in his own mouth and suck them like mints, savouring the salt of the gone.

Gradually the oil heated, burned deeper, mining for the core. The postmaster threw benzene on and the blaze began to crackle and reek. The onlookers stood with their palms out as the flames climbed and devoured each other. They stood warming themselves until the stench was too much and the flesh of the horse began to sizzle and slacken.

He did not see her leave. Did not see her hobbling off, shedding clothes then squatting. Neither he nor the rest of the men saw the steam rising from the cleft of her, her back chucking as it passed through. He did not see her on her haunches among the bald maples, petticoats in her hands, boots half-sunk in the snow. He did not see the red phlegm she took in her two cupped palms, along with a handful of snow. She stared into that clump for some time, then dropped on her bare haunches in the snow, gasped for a pain inside her and out. Malcolm did not see her turn twice as she buried all remnant of the blood that had passed through her, nor did he see her kick and pile fresh snow over what she'd left.

The seam in the horse's guts split and crackled and dribbled a brown sap. Beneath the flames, where the snow had melted, blackened roots coiled and twisted one on top of the other like a nest of still serpents. From the oil fields, a boom. A distant crack and blast and then a deep shudder in the earth. Men were shouting. The teamsters and the Methodist and the rest of them looked at one another, tried to gauge one another but he heard the world booming on, a sound like cannons shooting. People shouted for help, wailed for help, for flax, for horses, for barrels. Somewhere, gushers rose and roared.

Lise knocked a young pine as she limped back to the men. The trees above her swayed in the wind, dropped a fine dust of last night's snow.

"Bowels," she whispered, clutching her guts. He could see in her face that she was more than just sick. "I'm sorry," she said.

He didn't know what for but he knew what they had lost. He pulled her in, felt the new slack in her. Pulled her close and nested his face in her. The blazing horse glowed, reeked, shifted. The smell of burnt flesh on the air and he was embarrassed to feel his stomach turning in hunger. The men left one by one, nodded their goodbyes. In the fields, the clatter of hammering and drilling, the clanging of smiths.

"We should go," she said.

"Yes," he said, but she didn't move.

"I can't," she said, glancing down, then up at Sable.

"Right," he said. "Of course."

Gentle, he eased Lise up on the horse. Took Sable by the bridle and began the five-mile walk home.

SWAMP THINGS

MUM'S SPITTING HER CHEW into a double-double cup and I'm hovering my finger over Dawn's contact because it's been twenty-four hours and I said I wouldn't text again. It's mid-June—one more week before exams—and already the heat is thick, deep. Below the truck the pavement's a wobbly gelatine. The reporter on the radio is talking record Albertan wildfires. Beside me, Mum scoffs. "This shit again." A Captain Morgan's ghost rises off her breath. "Every year's a record, seems like. Gets tired." I shrug. Mum drools brown into the coffee cup. "Skipping school again today?"

I stare into my phone. "Protesting. And it's Thursday. Dad's picking me up, remember?"

"Who's Dawn?"

I clap a glance at Mum. "Don't look at my phone."

"Who pays the bill?" she says, grabbing for the phone as I slide it into my purse.

"Dad."

I hear honks and look up to see a black Mercedes SUV cruising out from a side street. It moves drunkenly, gleaming grille lurching and bobbing as drivers swerve to avoid it. A screeching mayhem of brakes then the bleating salvo as the Mercedes sparks over the barrier, trundles into the Esso station. It's rolling slow when it hits the vacant gas pump but still it folds the metal case. The box curling back to reveal a veinwork of black plastic tubes, a bundle of fibrillar orange wires.

Gas shoots up, a brown fountain.

Mum says, "Shit," and starts scrambling through her purse. The Mercedes howls, a sustained blare. Through the tinted windows the silhouette of the driver slumps against the wheel as gas geysers up from the sheared pump.

I cling to the handle, brace a palm against the dashboard. But there's no fire, no boom. Just the spurt of gasoline spraying ten feet into the air then crowning, turning, arcing down to land in a muddy spatter on the windshield. I think of childhood splash pads, the blue water creeping over huge plastic mushrooms.

Mum finds what she's looking for: peels back the foil and thumbs a Mentos into her mouth. The truck's engine keeps running though the traffic's stalled all around us. The Mercedes brays. "How about that," Mum says.

"It could still explode."

Mum scoffs, her breath sour with mint and rum.

"Any second. There's often a delay. There could be a fire in there, deep down."

I remember something Dad said once about internal combustion engines. How you can't see it but there's a fire burning all the time. "I've never really thought about it."

"What?"

"The gas. Where it comes from. That it's underneath us all the time."

"Comes from over there." Mum points down to Vidal, the citadel of the plants.

"It's beautiful," I say. "Beautiful and strange."

"That's sweet," Mum says, handing me the pack of Mentos. "Now hold this while I puke."

The traffic moves, finally, and we slide over the hill. I watch in the rear-view, waiting and waiting for a flash that doesn't come.

DAWN DOESN'T LIKE the word "weeds," doesn't believe in lawns. Dawn says "climate crisis," not "climate change." Dawn has delicate collarbones like a pair of fossilized skeleton wings. Once, when I touched them, she taught me their special name: "clavicles." Dawn keeps the ashes of her seven dead pets on the mantelpiece. Dawn has cinnamon skin and eyes that change colour at will. Dawn does not own a car, cycles two kilometres to work in all seasons, has a special bike with spiked tires for winter. In her front room, Dawn has a baby grand named "Retirement Project." Even as my English teacher, Dawn did not belittle my Alan Moore obsession. Dawn has two fanged scars along the bottom of her breasts from a reduction surgery in her twenties. Dawn's home teems with houseplants. Vined things curling off the piano, hanging below the skylight, crawling down the balustrade. She waters them tenderly with spray bottles, calls them by ever-changing literary names: Kafka, Virginia, Gertrude, Twain. Dawn makes me deep green cocktails that she calls "Swamp Thangs." Dawn keeps bees in her backyard, leaves the rest for wildflowers and pollinators, a raised bed for veggies. Dawn serves me curries jungled with cilantro from her garden, talks about the vegetal theory of oil origin. How the oil pumping through the Streamline refinery used to be life, plants and animals, microfauna and zooplankton stewed for hundreds of millions of years in gaseous chambers in the bottom of the earth. Dawn likes that she can talk to me, likes the way I listen, the way I "probe." Dawn and I are platonic in the *Symposium* sense, something about *erastes*. Dawn runs her thumb along my upper lip, tells me she loves the little blond hairs you can only see from kissing distance. When Dawn goes to the bathroom I open the mouth of the piano, run the backs of my fingers against the smooth white teeth.

LAST NIGHT I DREAMT the reactor. The one Dawn told me about, in Mumbai. A fortress of fission perched on the edge of the Indian Ocean. On the cusp of dream I saw the control rods trembling like the insides of a great organ. The core swollen, humming, the angry ocean swashing through the control room, swallowing reflectors and rods, a pus of uranium and beryllium frothing over the dancing sea. The works tumbling into the ocean, fish and krill and whales dying in one great neon flash. A burst fierce and final, devastating. And though I couldn't see what was revealed I knew that purple wave of light was both taint and revelation, a flowering doom.

The reactor churns through me as I arrive at school, chat with Deedee and Jenna about the Mercedes, the gasoline rain. The reactor hums and spins as I scout the halls for Dawn, fumble basketballs, hurt my thumb, stand in the back for dodgeball. As girls swirl out of the locker room after gym class I scroll through Twitter, watch the parade of *Bird Box* challenge videos, *Game of Thrones* memes, dead whales, starving polar bears, giraffes sliding onto the extinction list, another year of record temperatures, chunks of sea ice the size of Texas calving off Greenland, *Friends* personality quizzes, chubby bunny memes, *Stranger Things* spoilers.

Deedee and Jenna are talking about slogans for today's protest when Dad texts to confirm a 3:00 p.m. pickup. "Leaving at lunch. Lots to talk about. Podcast about sewage-to-energy."

"Good, thanks. Can't handle Mum today."

Dad sends three raised palm emojis with the Swiss flag. "Your mother's on board, correct?"

"Yes."

"Love you, Sapphire, see you soon."

"Who're you texting?" Jenna says, tossing a core in the garbage and mining her braces for apple skin.

"Your lover?" Deedee appears in my phone's reflection, bleached blond and starkly mascaraed. She grins, chomping a carrot. Deedee calls herself a non-denominational vegan atheist. She and Jenna know about Dawn, of course. They're my closest friends. We go to parties and climate protests.

Jenna adjusts her *Friends* sweater. "I heard she got fired?"

Deedee nods. "Something to do with the nail clippings?"

Jenna snorts: "No. Nails?"

Deedee shakes her feet, curls her toes: "Toenails. She clips them in class. Feeds her plants with them. She told us in grade ten. Gave a whole speech about the 'sigma of decay.'"

Stigma of decay.

"Then right in front of everyone she puts her feet up on the desk and—" Deedee mimes it. A kind of podiatric orgasm. Feet raised, pelvis swirling, hair thrown back.

"No." Jenna keels, keens. Giggling, tearing, cackling. "No. No. No. Stop. No."

I check my phone but there's no message. Just my lock-screen photo: a graphic image Dad sent me called "Future Toronto." The whole city flooded, condo buildings overgrown with vines and moss. The Rogers Centre converted to a giant greenhouse, sailboats cruising through the shallow waters of the lake. I imagine the black SUV roaring up that highway, devil-driven, screaming rubber, then soaring off the edge of that amputated highway in the sky.

"Yeah," Deedee says, jabbing her phone at me. "Sapphire was drooling for it." She does her porn voice again. "Tell me more, Miss Briar! More! More! More!"

WHEN YOU GROW UP in an Enchanted Castle of smog you tend to dislike home. When your mother is the lead operator in the Bio unit who brings home her bug-eyed boyfriend and stays up bingeing *Naked and Afraid* while filling the living room full of Sailor Jerry and Coke bottles, the bottoms swampy with chew-spit, you tend to prefer your dad although you can't stand his tiny condo in Etobicoke with the Queensway howling by. When you ride your tricycle along the train tracks looking out at the dozens of plants on either side of the river, you tend to covet Elsewhere. When the main reckless activity for teens is swimming across the sick-blue river to the refinery town on the other side, you dream of New York and Seattle and San Francisco. You dream of bare feet squelching through bogs, of double-helix rainbows, of a wonderworld that might have been painted by Jeff Jordan—frogs the size of skyscrapers and solar panel roses blooming in the desert. You dream of a woman, an older woman. A savvy woman who puts her phone face down for dinner. A woman who has watched the world wilt but has smuggled a smile. A woman who clips a piece of her pothos, hands it to you in a Mason jar. "Call her Pathos." A woman who breathes gardens, who knows we can't purge or clean up all this filth but maybe we can bend it into new ways of making.

LUNCH HAPPENS. Grocery store sushi happens. Sitting on a curb at the edge of the Loblaws parking lot with Deedee and Jenna listening to the blare of the 12:30 sirens happens. The same post-WWII alarm that tests every day at 12:30 to remind Sarnians that life is a form of PPE. That the air around us is a cauterized wound. That the leak is an ever-present threat, both norm and aberration. "The wonderhorn," Jenna mutters into her sushi.

Scrolling Twitter, Deedee lights up. "Holy shit," she says. "Awesome." Then she shares her findings: the Mercedes that crashed into the gas station was some Streamline office worker. Associate Director of Sustainability. He'd tweeted something about "extended beach season," a photo of himself windsurfing. Got a bunch of twitter hate and two weeks later, that is today, had a heart attack at the wheel. Streamline has put out a statement specifying that the event was not work-related.

Jenna snorts. "So fucking ironic."

Deedee goes on saying how great this is but my mind is back at the gas pump, the fluid pouring onto the windshield, pooling there like a strange squirming jellyfish, new colours blooming in a bursting, tentacled sun.

IN ART CLASS Mrs. Jha asks us to draw a rainbow into a scene of our choice. She strokes the sad sac of her stomach. Last year, she was flushed, swollen, giddy. She shows us some M. C. Escher slides, tell us to bend the real. "Whatever's been on your mind."

I cradle the pastels. What's been on my mind? Mrs. Jha likes my work for the wrong reasons. "Perfect neoclassical face." "Sophisticated linework." "Advanced perspective." Once Dawn saw me sketching a man on all fours, naked in the middle of the desert, solar panels chained to his sun-scarred back. Dawn called it a "curious blend of sacred and profane."

I decide against a Sailor Jerry bottle, against Mum leaking a rainbow of Skoal, against the reactor tumbling into the Indian Ocean, against Greta snorkeling in a garbage lagoon, against a dead sperm whale with an Evian intestine. I draw a man seen from behind pissing on the wall of a gas station. Above his head, an ad for bonus Air Miles. Beside him a giant novelty Coke bottle filled with actual Coke bottles. The stream of urine a sputtering pastel spectrum.

Mrs. Jha appears over my shoulder. "Office. Now."

Which means sitting on a scratchy maroon armchair watching the secretary clack away. Jenna texts me a string of toenail emojis and without looking the secretary tells me to put the phone away.

Principal Andrews calls me into her prison warden's office. Apparently the school was genuinely designed by a penitentiary architect. Andrews is mulleted, forty-something, built like a minifridge. A ribbon of fuchsia through her bone-bleached hair. High above us, there's a single dusty window, a square of seedy light trying to creep in. And there's a small dry jade in a black plastic pot. Its petals white and wilting.

"So," Andrews says. She's holding my artwork, examining it. She pinches it by one corner, dangles it away from her face. A soiled thing.

"I followed the instructions."

Andrews drones about principles, the spirit of education. I watch the light change in the window, dust turn to ash on the windowsill. "I'm going to have to call your mother."

"Good luck. Four off. She works in the Bio unit. She'll be neck-deep in Skoal and Sailor Jerry."

Andrews sets my piece down on the side of her desk. "Your father then."

"Driving in from Toronto. Still two hours away."

"All right," she says. "I'm writing an email to your mother. And you'll go back to class for today and you'll be amenable. Correct?"

I swallow, nod. Dawn. She howls my blood.

Andrews bobs the painting. "You should know that this kind of work goes beyond distasteful. It's—"

She gags for the word. Spits it like a hairball: "*Obscene*."

I think down towards my pocket, my phone. Its cobalt pulse. Dawn's thumbs, pattering sweetly. Dawn saying that she gets it, she understands. Dawn calling me baby, Sapphy, Sappho.

I tell Andrews that yes I understand why I'm being suspended for the rest of the day and tomorrow. I smile and nod and tell her of course I'll be back on Monday with an attitude adjustment. When she tells me to go I ask her if she minds.

She straightens. "What is it?"

"I'm just wondering about Miss Briar. Any idea when she might be back?"

Andrews rubs her forehead, asks if that's my business, if I'm even Miss Briar's student this semester. "No." I pause, stare up at the window, the parched jade. "But there's Reach for the Top, and it's just not the same with Mr. Arsenault as it is with Dawn."

She squints at me, then over me. "Dawn? Does Miss Briar ask you to call her that?"

Shit. The window pulses, throbs. The room sours. "No. Sorry, no, I just—"

Andrews nods, slow. "She's ill," she says. "Is all I can say."

I cross the street and wait for Dad outside the waist-high jungle of the abandoned Libcor refinery, sun thumping down. Nothing from Dawn. Parched crabgrass, dandelions, a clutch of lupins, a few red trilliums. Names Dawn has taught me. On the rusted scrap of chain-link a grey cardinal alights, around him a coterie of white butterflies. An old rusted sign that reads, LIBCOR PROPERTY DO NOT ENTER.

I'm texting with Deedee—*she actually said "attitude adjustment"*—when the study about 2048 slides onto my phone. The sour clutch of the afternoon heat and Deedee's talking plans for tomorrow night. Plans to go to the house of some old guy they know, a landscaper with a pool. I click through to the article, the author citing a Dalhousie study, CNN stating as if I needed to hear again that "the apocalypse is coming sooner than you think."

DAD CALLS HIMSELF a shit man, which usually gets the desired eyebrow raise. Which invites his follow-up about his job managing the City of Toronto's biggest water treatment facility. Then the story of how he started off working the boards at Streamline, ran poly broilers for twenty years. Hydrobonds, piston pumps, valve monkeys. What he generally does not mention is meeting Mum in the Bio unit. A polyurethane romance. The two of them making eyes across the hangar, bodies glowing as the dials whirled and spun. Mum sashaying through her checks, the lines above throbbing naphtha-fat, dials whirring and wheeling. Dad was all set for retirement when he started to talk to the union people. Resulting in a generous severance package and though Dad wasn't ready to stop working he was ready to sever with Mum so he moved to Toronto. Crunched and sluiced and filtered his way to the top of the city's new mansion of sewage. Meaning now he has to drive back to Sarnia to pick up his Alan Moore fan-girl child every second weekend. A three-hour drive with no traffic and there's always traffic. Dad always says we've got to stop doing this, driving and flying. I know he's right and I know we keep doing it.

IN THE PRIUS, AC on full and barely working, Dad asks about Mum, about home. I'm watching two women in the car behind us. A little red Kia. Twenties or thirties. The woman in the passenger seat has short hair and tattoos, a white T-shirt. She's talking and talking, her hands pumping up and down. Bringing a coffee to her lips but never drinking from it because she's too excited about what she's saying. Smiling, then getting heated, turning to look at the other woman. They could be lovers or colleagues or friends but what matters is that they are together. Talking and feeling together in their rolling room of glass and steel.

"Mum's great," I say. "Planning another trip to Varadero so at least I'll have the house to myself?" I don't mention the graveyard of Coke bottles, one of them tipped over, leaking black sludge on the brown carpet.

Dad laughs into the windshield. "Heavy-duty Suzy," he says.

"'Sleep when I'm dead.'"

We pass farm after farm and Dad tells me about sludge energy. Farms possible because of ancient swamps. The soil so rich Dawn says we should not be building houses here. China is smart enough to know that this is not a question of values anymore; it's about survival, economically prudent. "Can you imagine pouring sewage into the ocean? All that wasted energy, precious rot?" Farm, farm, windmill. Watford, Strathroy, Middlesex. After Waterloo: malls and malls, roads and malls and underpasses. We roll and brake through the pavement belt. Dawn says it's so big and dense you can see it from space.

Dawn. I don't check my phone. Then I do.

Around Woodstock we get stuck behind a big white pickup, the driver drifting into the shoulder then the middle lane and back. His head tilted down just a little, just enough.

"Fucking texters," Dad says. He looks at me, winks: "Whoops."

Outside London we see an SUV on fire across the median. Sam Cooke's singing about teenage girls, Dad humming along, when we enter the sea of brake lights, the traffic gently slowing. There is no obstruction on our side of the highway but the vehicles sag as drivers turn their heads to look across the barrier. The silver SUV is fully immersed in a flame that flickers gaseous, liquid in the heat. There's an ambulance and a fire truck, some police cars with their lights flashing. There's one lane closed but the cars just pull around, squeeze through the obstruction, blast into the straightaway. For a moment I see the seats inside, each one a tower of flame. And then we're gone, taking a corner. In the rear-view the SUV keeps burning, shards of heat through the shredded sky.

The world blurs and lurches by. Cineplex, Costco, water tower, Cineplex. Dad starts talking about jellyfish cities, whole cities powered by jellyfish, the leftover protein harvested for food. In the core of the city, Dad says, there would be a giant tub full of jellies, a throbbing furnace, and on the outside a great translucent computational wall. A kind of Siri membrane that would hold information in and filter the air. Dad chuckles, pleased with himself. "You could probably store information in the jellies' cells."

"So we'd steal all their energy? Make jellyfish slaves?"

"No. I don't know."

Dad's trying to think around this, wincing past the traffic to the parade of malls and gyms and suburbs when my phone chirps. Can't be Dawn. Jenna or Mum forgetting where I am. As long as I don't look there is still a possibility. But I'm looking, of course.

Everything all right stuck in intensive care no cause for alarm.

I start to text back. Find myself gushing about Mum, about Sailor Jerry, about the Toyota and the wildfires and 2048. I delete it all. Go for a question: *What happened?*

I wait. Watch three blinking dots appear and vanish. No cause for alarm.

Maybe another angle: *Should I come see you?*

Or another: *What happened?*

Do you need help? Are you all right? Are you alone?

I'm coming.

Finally, she responds: *Please don't.*

Malls spin by. Cinemas rise from the pavement—towering, monstrous, gone. Gas stations flash and flicker. SUVs burn, crash. Gasoline rises, pours. Traffic. More traffic. I stare at the phone. Put it in the glove compartment. Stare at the glove compartment.

"What's wrong?" Dad asks.

Without thinking: "Dawn."

"Who's Dawn?"

"My English teacher from last semester."

"Miss Briar? You text with a teacher?"

"She's not teaching me anymore so it's okay?"

Dad's jaw goes tight. He thinks for a long time. "I'm not sure it is. What do you know about the legality?"

"Not much."

Dad stares hard into the windshield. "Is this sexual?"

"Ew."

"Sorry—romantic?"

"No. No." I stare at the console's trove of gum wrappers and parking slips. Dad knows I've dated guys. He doesn't know there are women too, but I know he'd be cool about it. "Do you believe me?"

Dad considers the skyline, then the dashboard. "I trust you."

I smile. Open the glove compartment, then close it. Dad smiles his you-can-talk-but-no-pressure smile. A sign announces that we're entering the Green Belt as three lanes become four, then eight. I start telling him about Dawn, about 2048, about the strangled poisoned ocean, about the dead right whales in the St. Lawrence and the giraffes sliding onto the endangered species list while everyone clicks through to the next Kardashian meme.

Dad takes my hand. Reaches over and puts his hand on my thigh and says baby, baby. Dad says my poor sweet girl. Dad says he's so so sorry and he just doesn't know what else to say. He says he's sorry but sometimes the world just feels broken and there's nothing we can do but we have to hope, don't we?

And then I'm telling him about Dawn, how I know all this because of her and she's the only one who cares about what I think, how she called my art "sacred and profane" because she gets it, she really fucking gets it. Mrs. Jha will never get it and then I'm just saying her name, not sure what I'm sad about anymore, just babbling, "Dawn, Dawn, Dawn."

Dad takes my hand, says again that he's sorry, that it hurts, that he knows it hurts and he's felt hurt like that before, that he feels awful for me and he doesn't know if there's anything more he can do.

The lake comes into view, flaunt of a million glinting waves. Cyclists lean over handlebars. Mothers push strollers. Windsurfers curl for the horizon.

DAD AND I WATCH *Grizzly Man* again and he makes me hot chocolate, goes out for Häagen-Dazs and hands me the bowl gently, with his eyes down. "Fair trade," he says. I stand up and give him a long deep hug. "Thanks," I tell him.

After the movie, Dad snores on the couch and I lie awake listening to the ghosts of the Queensway. There's a sound barrier but it doesn't work well enough, and from Dad's fourth-floor apartment it makes the highway below look sci-fi and military. A moon base. If you listen close you can hear the cars through the glass. If you close your eyes, they sound like far-off people. People wailing, moaning. People that could have done more but never enough. Three years ago, when Dad and Mum broke up, I had a choice. I didn't like Toronto, wasn't big on Queen West or dreadlocked sub-urbanites or TTC tokens. Dad works too much anyway, and my friends are in Sarnia, and when I think of Elsewhere it's a lot of places but it's not the fourth floor of an Etobicoke condo building looking down onto the grey walls of the Queensway, the perpetual Christmas of throbbing tail lights.

Trying to sleep, I keep seeing the flame-crazed SUV. The steel frame beneath the enflamed roof, drops of liquid metal starting to form. The bare bones of the vehicle melting into the concrete.

DAD WAKES ME UP wagging his *World's Best Dad* mug. He tells me sorry but he's got to cut the weekend short. Surprise invite for a conference in California. Connections, a "game-changer." He winks: "Drop you off on the way."

We stop at the office, which means me in the car staring at the plant. A huge concrete tower, squat red-brick buildings. I did a tour once, saw the squat tanks and the soil rows, the riddled white pipelines connecting it all. Beryllium-yellow cyclists wheel up Lakeshore, turn down to Leslie Spit. Watching them, I remember Dawn's story about the old landfill of Front Street, how all the new waterfront is built on top of it. A whole lakeshore built on garbage. Past the plant, couples play volleyball on the man-made beach.

Dawn in her kitchen wearing her gardening gloves. Dawn putting on her apiary suit for me, naked underneath. The two of us giggling on the bed. Light slanting down. Dawn saying it would be better if I didn't shave it. Dawn counting the freckles on my legs, walking her fingers up my thighs.

Dad taps the glass. Climbs in short of breath and hands me a travel mug with no lid. I look into the brown grunge he brews with the office French press. "Sludge energy," he says, starting the car.

"For me or you?"

He grins, pulls the wrong way onto Lakeshore. "Both."

I sip the murk, chew the grits into my teeth. I make Dad promise that he won't tell Mum about the Dawn thing. He raises his palms. "Switzerland." We drive on in silence, listen to radio ads for mattresses, McDonald's, Virgin Mobile. We take the 403 back and once we're past Hamilton I fall into a thin and lurching sleep.

WHEN MUM AND DAD were still together, we used to talk a lot about the whale shark migration, about going there as a family. Mum would thumb through hotel and car rental options and I would struggle just to imagine that you could swim with giants on the Ningaloo Reef. Somewhere off the Yucatán Peninsula, there are whale sharks drifting through the frigid deeps. Creatures that are thirty feet long and weigh twenty tons. Creatures with three hundred rows of teeth. Pelagic filter feeders that dive to six thousand feet, descending into the midnight zone, where light has never spilled or seeped through the endless fathoms. Creatures quietly brooding in the depths while the human spasm storms and fizzles. Whale sharks diving through the coldest corridors of the ancient unseen sea.

GUTS ROTTEN FROM HUNGER and coffee, I walk through the emergency entrance, drift through the bright sliding doors. Dad dropped me across from the school, turned the corner as the city bus pulled up. Inside the hospital, the AC roars fast and cool. Coke machines wiggle and whir. I don't check in, just roam the halls, nurses glancing strange.

I pass infants, pregnant women in wheelchairs, boys with broken legs. Everywhere white walls, sad sapped people. I peek into the doors of the sick, the elderly. I see a woman squatting fully naked, moaning like an airplane, the keg of her stomach flexing, rippling. I keep telling myself the hospital can't be that big. No cause for alarm. No cause for alarm alarm alarm.

Her voice, her laugh. A laugh like summer thunder.

I pull back a curtain to find a fit nurse hovering beside Dawn's bed. Dawn lies back, rigid, face and hands bandaged. Seeing me, the nurse pulls her hand back suddenly. Holds one dangling in the other. There are flowers all around the bed but what I see is Dawn's red swollen skin. A horror of red up her neck, on her temples, her lips. Her eyes a drained green, the flesh bloated around them. The nurse looks at me hard. Holds my gaze and finally leaves.

Once we're alone I whisper: "Dawn."

She winces. "Please. Sorry but—" She looks towards the hallway. Red sores peek out from her bandages, jewel the mounds of her clavicles.

"Sorry. Would you like me to call you Miss Briar?"

"Don't be dramatic. Should I call your mother?"

I laugh. "It's not fair. You can't just—"

"Sorry," she hisses, holding up her bandaged hands. "It's hard to communicate right now." She changes her tone, speaks louder: "Did you want to discuss an assignment?"

"No." I shake my head. "No no no no you don't do that. You can't do that to me this is fucked I deserve things."

I reach for her hand but she pulls back.

"The bees," I shout. "The fucking bees. I knew they were a bad idea, a terrible idea. I know the world needs pollinators. But not so close, not right there. Your poor, poor body." I reach for her skin and she flinches again.

"Oh hon," she says.

"Don't hon me."

"I'm sorry, Sapphire. What a mess. It was bad. It's always been a bad idea."

"So it's over?"

She snorts. "Please. It was two afternoons."

I glare at the red wreckage of her. "Just don't tell me you didn't feel it."

She smiles, clucks. Nods like no, she didn't. Like I'm so naive. Like I'll understand when I'm older. She glances around the room, out into the hallway. "It's my fault. I gave the wrong impression." She's using her teacher voice. "I hope you understand. I hope you'll be discreet."

"Okay." I nod, spin, walk.

THE PROTEST IS ME and Jenna and Deedee. There's another heat warning. Risk of smog in Sarnia. Children and the elderly and people with breathing issues advised to stay indoors. Kids amble back from lunch, join us for a vape, then head home or to class. Deedee is HOW DARE YOU and Jenna is NO PLANET B and I'm DYING SLOW 4 STATUS QUO. We sit on the stairs. We post bored selfies of ourselves with air filtration masks on, stacks jabbing up through the background. We look online at massive crowds in London and Berlin and it feels like we're part of something. Something huge and distant. We put our phones away and it's gone.

Dawn came back to school two weeks after I visited. She's got some scarring around her neck, a little below her ears. She nods politely in the halls when I pass. I want her to ignore me, to shun me. I want her to scream, to flail her arms. Instead, her acid courtesy.

Jenna takes out a bottle of SPF 60. "Supposed to be forty-five with the humidex."

"Fuck that." Deedee snorts.

I scroll through my messages, wince at the seven I sent to Dawn. I stare at her response. *Please don't.* I wonder what it meant, what she felt when she sent it, if ending it was a job thing or a for-your-own-sake thing or if it had just gone sour for her.

Deedee starts talking about tonight. A pool party. A litre of Russian Prince. We watch the rugby girls churn into a bus.

A cloud moves, and I adjust my sunglasses. "It's not enough, is it?"

Deedee perks. "A litre of vodka?"

"No. This." I wiggle my sign. "The non-violence, Greta, the whole shtick. It's exhausting. Feels like you're screaming into a toilet."

Jenna and Deedee nod, eyes hazy. The rugby girls pull away, and reveal a cycling Dawn. Everything spandex. Her long legs. Hamstrings like salmon pulsing through the river. Dawn nods hello but doesn't stop.

I see Deedee giving me the horse-eye. Then she touches my wrist. "What happened?"

"Nothing."

"I know I chirp you," she says. "But we can talk about it."

"No." I stand up, turn towards home. "We really can't."

Deedee tugs my shorts. "You're coming tonight. I know this handsome Russian prince. Got to meet him."

"I don't know."

As I'm walking away Jenna shouts, "Let's make some memories!"

Deedee: "And obliterate them!"

THE LAST TIME I saw her, Dawn and I had gone for a walk by the river. There were sailboats out, and motorboats. Across the river Port Huron winked and overhead transport trucks spun through the road in the sky. We looked down at the refineries and she told me again about the vegetal theory, how all that oil used to be life. Of course that got me onto the *Swamp Thing* comics, the merits of the Moore version over the Pasko and Collins. Dawn told me about the resonances she remembered from my essay on floronic monstrosity. Residues of Frankenstein's creature, the Hulk, King Kong. I told her what I was always interested in was Moore's mythology, the Parliament of Trees. The plant-protecting elementals that lived on this planet before humans. What happened, I explained, was synthesis. In the story, when a creature dies in flames it merges with the earth and joins the parliament. Hence Eyam, Bog Venus, and Swamp Knucker the dinosaur. Dawn went pensive, watching smoke bloom through the charcoal sky. "So what does that have to do with oil?" she said, and I didn't like it because she was using her teacher voice but I knew what she meant before she said it. This oil-filled city, she said, this oil-thick land. It's nothing but plant and animal bodies, biovegetal matter. Ancient life burning through this weeping wildfire world.

I **WALK AROUND** the school and in the back doors. I go through the basement, turn up a quiet hallway. I should not know she has a prep period, an empty classroom. I should not know that she keeps her spandex shorts on underneath her jeans, that there's a loam of cooling sweat in the pout of her lower back as she sits on the ergonomic swivel chair she rolled on foot from Staples.

"Hello," she says, straightening. She wears foundation now, though she doesn't need to. No scar could mar her.

"Is there…" She sniffs. Takes a drink of pomegranate soy milk smoothie. Goes loud: "There's no Reach for the Top today."

A tall boy skateboards through the blurry window, his hair like a blond cactus.

"I'm tired," I tell her. "I can't do this. I don't think I can—"

In the hallway, someone's phone sings mournful autotune.

"Listen." She puts her hand across the desk and leaves it there, looking me hard in the eye. The welts climb her forearms, red and cystic. Her eyes hold strong. Embers green and throbbing. "I need this. For me, for us. I need you to be strong, to keep it together. And maybe, after things quiet down."

"Maybe what?"

She nods fast. Puts her hands in her knees and squeezes them together. Inhales without looking at me. "Maybe once you graduate."

"Maybe what?"

The tall boy tries a kickflip, board scattering through the parking lot. Brakes screech. Dawn twirls her plastic throne.

I'M HOLDING PATHOS, stroking the cool green sunburst of her leaves, when Mum knocks on my bedroom door. I set the plant on the windowsill and open the door to Mum doing her three-drink doting face. Virgil's calling from the next room. "Suze! Saltwater crocodiles!" I'm guessing also nudity and fear.

Mum walks in, sits on the bed. "What's going on with your teacher?"

Dad. Fuck.

"Nothing."

Rows of Alan Moore spines stare at us from my bookshelves. Cartoon Heather Locklear gazes sultry from the *Return of Swamp Thing* poster. Thighs peeking out of her flowy red dress. A thought bubble: *Why can't men be more like plants?*

Mum inches closer, her weight on the bed sucking me into her. "You call your teacher Dawn? I found another old message from your principal."

So potentially not Dad.

Virgil, howling: "Suze, you got to see this!" The volume on the TV goes up.

"Hold on," Mum shouts to the door. Then she turns to me, half drunk and tender. "This Miss Briar. Is she the one filling your brain with all these swamp things?"

"*Swamp Thing.*"

"Whatever." She breathes, steadies. Looks to the wall and back to me. "Should I be concerned?"

"Sounds like you'd rather not."

"What?"

"Be concerned."

Mum shrinks, then grows. Her face clenches. "Don't get smart with me." She skulks away muttering. I stay where I am, listening.

My phone dings. Deedee. "Russian Prince? Dad got Leafs tickets."

I walk by Virgil and Mum giggling on the couch, both holding Coke bottles, spitting into them in sync.

As I slip into my flats Mum growls, "Where you going?"

I tell her a walk and see you tomorrow. She shouts something at the closing door but doesn't rise from the couch.

ME AND DAWN were turning her compost heap. I held a pitchfork, which was as close as I wanted to get, but she was on her knees on the tarp we'd spread, hands deep in the sappy black. There were eggshells and hunks of banana peel, stray bits of white plastic, a throb of insects. From the far corner of the yard the bees buzzed around their hive. "The thing about compost," Dawn was telling me, "is that it needs heat. The right mixture of greens and browns otherwise it'll stagnate. You need it to heat up, help the rot kick in." I told her about Moore's mythology, the Parliament of Trees. The plant-protecting elementals that lived on this planet before humans. How when a creature died in flames it merged with the earth and joined the Parliament. She giggled like cute. Then she paused, put her nose close to the pile and sniffed. She leaned forward and took a fat handful, let some spill through her fingers, dusting the tarp. "Here," she said, "touch it." I didn't want to. Approached cautiously, fearfully. Stood there panting before the rich sour smells, the drone of bee and street, the vibrations from the plants. I felt the world heating, seeking its origins, longing for the swamp. Dawn worked the ink-dark compost in her hands. Then, grinning wild, she smeared it over her cheeks and chin. "It's rich," she said, giddy. "So damn rich." I knelt on the tarp and put a single finger into the dense earth, felt the astonishment of its heat. As I pulled my finger back wet and warm, the black slime clung on. Laughing, Dawn came over, took my hand, plopped my brown slick finger into her mouth and sucked the rot off. "Attagirl," she said, triumphant. Then she guided my hand deeper into the pile. Sunk it up to the wrist, then the forearm. I let it happen, let it feel good.

I WALK SLOW to Deedee's through a mean-fisted heat. Over the river the sun's waning, but its memory sings through the pavement. Mum texts to ask where I'm going. She needs to know for real. Deedee's dad's apartment is a dank oubliette of free weights and cracked leather couches. The walls are covered with fishing photos and hockey memorabilia, a signed Gretzky jersey. Deedee sits forward on the couch, flourishing the plastic bottle of Russian Prince.

"We call this the Feminine Hygiene Bloodstream Project." She opens the bottle and starts to pour into a mixing bowl on the glass coffee table. Inside the bowl there are three unwrapped tampons. She mixes screwdrivers while we wait, watching the tampons bloat, the room sharp with vodka smell.

I stare at the near-empty bottle of Russian Prince, thinking through the plastic bottle and into the clear liquid, thinking about the corn or wheat or soy that made it. The sugars slowly breaking down, finally becoming ethanol. I think about refinement, about willowy plants drinking sunlight in Russian fields, fluid sintering in great steel vats and gradually clarifying. A corrosive astonishment of clear.

"Should we shoot some?"

I see a rifle, a wolf stalking the grain rows in a Russian field.

Deedee wags a little silver shot glass. Jenna nods and Deedee fills the glass, flicking her black hair back as she drinks. We watch the bowl, stare into our phones. Jenna tells us about her cousins who're going to be at the party, and the older guys with trucks.

"It's time," Deedee says. She pulls a tampon out of the bowl, holds it dripping over her hand as she heads to the bathroom. She comes back grinning. "That'll put some hair on your tits."

Jenna stands up. "Hair on your fucking clit." She takes the bowl to the bathroom, brings it back to me with one tampon remaining. "Your hygiene, Your Highness."

I sit on the toilet next to the pebble-glassed sink, wondering if either of the other girls faked it. We stumble to the party, the strange tickle of the vodka perking through my bloodstream. We walk through the driveway and into the floodlit backyard. A sea of tattoos and flat-brimmed caps, of boys crushing tall cans. A bunch of deep fryers and plates of wings and cheese-filled mushrooms laid out on picnic tables next to full ashtrays. There are crews of older guys, beer-bellied plant workers.

An old guy with brown buck teeth smiles at us. "IDs please."

"Come on," Deedee says. We clamber up the side of the raised pool and sit teetering on the edge of it, letting the warm water gush our ankles. Deedee sits beside an ogre of a hockey player who lets her bend into him for a few minutes before asking how old she is. The host comes around with a tray of LED-white shooters, calls them "Android Blood."

I hold the pool tight, the booze whizzing through me faster and faster. Guys come up and talk to me and I smile back mean until they leave. I stagger to the spinning bathroom and pull the tampon out. Wait there clawing at peeling yellow tiles. The floor around the toilet a sticky yellow nimbus. I clutch at the tap, the room teetering, listing. I spill water on my arm and chest and then get some in my mouth, cue the hot relief of vomit.

I drink more water and emerge, zinging sober, to find the hockey ogre shouting, addressing the crowd. People are gathering around him. He's peeling off his clothes, shouting about the river, about swimming to another country.

Deedee and Jenna trade glances. I can see that they want to. Someone shouts about the current. The current pulling south, into the river mouth. The currents beneath us, the currents in the pipeline, the currents, currents, occurrence.

On the walk down, in a crowd thick with tall cans and laughter and squealing girls, I fall to the back of the crowd thinking of the poison humming through me. Thinking of the closed office door. Of Dawn leaning over to look at my essay, her jeans, the feel of her thigh-flesh beneath them. Of how she ended it, how not to treat a person. I get the secrecy thing, get that it's complicated but wrong, still wrong, has to be wrong.

We approach the river, the rocky downtown beach where kayakers launch and swimmers cool their ankles by day. The stark light of the refinery plays on the black water as men peel their shirts, girls jumping one-legged, caught in their jeans. The hockey player sprints at the river fully naked and leaps out over the concrete blocks. When his head comes up you can see the full moon of his bald spot.

Deedee grabs me by the wrist. Drunk, swaying gently in the concrete. The strange thing is she's smiling as she says it. "What happened anyway? With you and Dawn?"

I swallow. Think *nothing*.

An old photo of Dawn pinned on her corkboard, arm in arm with a man. Halloween, dressed as poison ivy. Green lipstick, green hair.

Deedee's eyes glow fierce. Her mascara chunking on her lashes. She grips my wrist harder. "You should do something. You're not the only one."

Jenna's peeling her top off, then her shorts. Her butt cheeks catching moonlight as she stands knee-deep, shivering. Deedee close behind her and I'm not sure what else to do, not sure what I want so I swim. The hockey player is in the lead, his huge arms splashing reckless but pulling through strong. The water cool on me, the lights dancing, quivering.

I swim with friends and strangers, swim and swim, boats honking in the distance, refineries glowing on both sides of the river, the lights globbing over the water. Everyone hooting and shouting and then going quieter. Steady breathing. The odd gasp.

Deedee comes close and we stop for a moment, treading water. "You all right?"

I tell her yeah, I'm fine. I turn onto my back and watch the clouds whish and loaf through the dark sky. A few dull stars wink. There are voices calling, giggling, shouting. Quieter and quieter. When I turn back over I see them far away and shrinking. Arms wheeling and splashing into the blinking horizon. I see the closest person waving. I have to squint to see her but yes it's Deedee and then she's shouting, shrill voice keening over the water, distant and desperate: "What are you waiting for?"

I pause there treading water in the open river. Halfway between two shores, two countries, two smouldering towns. And then I'm sinking, seal-like, into the darkness. Holding my breath and dropping, descending into the river's black. I open my eyes, watch the lights play on the surface thinking into Deedee's question. Into it and with it and through it.

Then I turn, pivot slowly. Reach out and pull.

I arrive panting at the beach, heave myself up. I find my shorts, my top, then mount the hill. A lost and lonely creature shedding water on the shore.

I'M WAITING OUTSIDE the office when Principal Andrews squeaks down the hall with a Booster Juice in her hand, GoodLife bag bouncing off her hip. It's just her, no office staff yet. She's got yoga pants on, bright sneakers.

In the past week, there was a super-flare, a major meltdown, and a death at the plant. Mum won't tell me what's going on, but I heard her muttering something about taxidermy. More and more, it feels like we're hitting the edge of something. More and more, I picture the plants rusting out, sprouting tangles of vines, carbon steel Medusas crawling slowly into the river.

Principal Andrews squints, surprised. "Hi?"

I just look at her. The keys are shaky in her hands but she lets me in. Sets her gym bag in the corner and boots up the computer. The window has been dusted, and the jade plant is gone. Another hot day and the window is a throbbing yellow ember.

Andrews takes a sip of her smoothie and asks if there's something she can do.

I take my phone out, scroll through the pictures. Hover on the one of a woman in an apiary suit.

She sighs. "Right."

She tells me to send her the evidence.

"Right now?"

"Yes."

"All of it?"

She gives me the email address and I scroll through my phone. Watch the colour in the windows change as I send her the messages and photos. She asks if I'm willing to provide a statement. I say yes and she tells me fine, that's all for now. Then she gives me a look. An almost smile. A kind of lip-bit recognition.

On the way through the empty office I pass an unemptied garbage bin, see the jade plant sitting near the top. It looks parched and wilted, but salvageable. I reach in through the coffee cups and muffin wrappers, the milk-brown rills of yesterday's double-double. In the black plastic pot the soil is dry and chalky, the roots impacted at the edges. Pulling it closer, I see that the plant is diseased, studded with gnarled black growths. Gently, I set it back. Lowering the pot into the plastic bag, I imagine the landfill it will settle in, the mound of vhs tapes and diapers and dog shit that will be its final garden. A heap of busted plastic at the end of an endless world.

OILGARCHS

26/06/2019. We are the N95 children. We are the purifiers, the carbon sinks. We see the world through polypropylene lenses, swim vinyl pools. We are weary with Oilgarchs—their wheezing desperation, their anaesthesia of greed. We expose the euphemism of acquisition, refuse the acid reign of Western law and knowing. We breathe the air of Vidal Street; we remember the evacuation of Bluewater Village; we trawl among the intersex fish. We remember the toxic blob, the spilled detergent, the skull-and-crossbones signs at the river's fringe. We know about the land theft, the burial grounds quaking hydraulic, their chemical cathedral. We know about Health Canada refusing the studies. Zebra mussels shamming the water blue.

I'M THINKING OF the brain in the jar when Sapphire flips her newly bleached hair and sets the Ringwraith masks on the table. "I've identified the target," she says. It's an annual tradition to dine and dash on the last day of classes. Extra special on the last day of grade twelve. Jenna's been calling it "the last last day." The brain was found in a Mason jar in the cargo of a transport truck heading across Blue Water Bridge. They showed it on TV—blue hands holding the clear jar and inside the grey flub of brain wrapped in paper towel and bubble packing.

"Speak now," Sapphire says, miming handgun. "Or forever hold your piece."

"Target?" Jenna scoffs into her menu. "Don't be dramatic."

"Target," Sapphire repeats, brandishing the three masks and glaring at Jenna, at me. I watch out the window as a blue jay settles on a teenage maple. One of the city-planted trees, a black plastic cast around its trunk, leaves withering because it hasn't rained in weeks. Or because of the street behind it, snarling with motorbikes and pickup trucks.

"Who is it?" I ask.

"Not here." Sapphire adjusts her T-shirt, cropped primly ragged. "We're meeting the contact tomorrow."

Jenna scoffs. "You mean your cousin?"

Sapphire snaps: "This is serious."

"All right, Mission Impossible."

The server skulks over and Sapphire asks for spicy tuna. I get cucumber maki. Jenna squints at the server: "What's a dumpwing?" He tells her it's like a cross between a dumpling and a chicken wing. Jenna stares back. Orders edamame and red curry. "There's fusion," Jenna says. "And then there's *con*fusion." Plates arrive. Jenna stirs her curry, finds mostly potatoes. Sapphire worries her chopsticks, avoids Jenna's eyes.

"Look," Jenna says. "I'm out."

Sapphire snorts, eyes the ceiling. "Of course."

"I'm not sure you get what you're doing. This stuff needs to be organized."

"I'm tired of peaceful," Sapphire says. "It's not doing anything."

"This will be worse. All of this falls back on the community, on Aamjiwnaang."

Before she says it, Sapphire glances at me for confirmation. "We're allies."

"Sure. Congratulations."

Jenna pushes her chair back. "Deedee?" She looks at me like am I coming? I know I should, know she's right. But I'm watching her leave.

"Fuck her," Sapphire says. "Better this way. Cleaner. Right?"

I slide the last piece of maki into my mouth. The tip of the chopstick comes out broken, rough. There's no splinter, but I taste the tiny cut in my mouth, a fissure in the dark of me.

27/06/2019. We are sodden with sadness, beleaguered with elegy, sick with the thesaurus of useless hope. Change, emergency, crisis. Terminology does not change death. Does not change gas, CO_2 levels, methane and benzene and hydrogen sulfide in our water, our brains, our air, our bones. Carbon taxes as if we might tithe ourselves free. We know that it's not just us, not just here. We know that everyone lives in Chemical Valley. That there is always a refinery around the corner, a reactor in the closet. We live in an age of Militant Toxicity. Death by Chemical is mundane, banal. Where are our furies?

DAD GRUNTS AND creaks his weight bench, his neck flexed, meat-red. He swills Coors between reps, pretends not to glance at himself in the hall mirror. I'm reading about the target, Streamline's V.P. Operations. He tweeted something tasteless about the toxic blob becoming the city's mascot. Deleted it quickly but there are screenshots. Sapphire also sent me a note she wants to post after. "We need to claim it," she said. "Or there's no point."

Dad rises for water and I stare out the window, thinking about the brain. Last week I saw a diver on local TV, a former navy officer who scubas under the bridge every day talking about the astonishing things he finds: a Petoskey stone net sinker from Stone Age fishing, a human skull from a wrecked nineteenth-century schooner.

Jenna calls from her auntie's house. "You know we don't, right?"

I walk past Dad, trying not to hustle through the hall, down the steps, onto the sidewalk. "What?"

"'We all live in Chemical Valley.' That sounds like a Sapphire line."

"Well. Is she wrong?"

"There are degrees, Deedee. There's wealth. There's privilege, proximity. There's living next to the golf course and there's having the plants in your fucking backyard, on your burial ground."

On the front lawn of the building, squirrels chatter through a yellow shock of grass. The air is thick with the particular reek of refineries in summer. "Smells like money," Dad likes to say.

Jenna sighs. "It sucks, all right. You know I love Sapphire, and I know she's got her own shit to deal with. But she won't do it without you."

"We're doing it."

"Then do it right. You get in touch with the police. You need liaisons. You don't hurt people. There are already people doing this work. You need to listen."

"It's all planned. We're sending a message."

"It won't change anything."

She hangs up, which is when I see the bones. In the stomped concrete, a mash of white, barely recognizable. The remnant of a claw, the crushed snarl of a tail. A rat decomposing, feeding the stone.

27/06/2019.
January 2011: Leviathan leaks undisclosed quantity of mercaptan.
July 2013: Libcor spills 7,000 gallons of oil into the St. Clair River.
December 2014: TJX spills 50 kilograms of ammonium carbonate.
February 2015: Polymax spills 113 litres of corrosive materials.
March 2016: Polymax spills 262 kilograms of ammonium nitrate.
September 2016: Streamline spills 63 kilograms of benzene.
March 2017: Polymax spills 331 kilograms of sulphides.
*September 2017: Libcor spills 104 kilograms of benzene/toluene
    xylene.*
April 2019: Libcor flare spills into gaseous ditch.
*June 2019: Streamline leaks unknown quantity of hydrogen
sulfide.*

YOU GROW UP right angles. You grow up with Jenna, two toothy girls biking around the river's fringe, regarding its twinkle, swan diving off the dock, learning every last word of *The Little Mermaid*. Together, you spend afternoons flopping around the house, tying towels around your legs, singing,

"Poor Unfortunate Souls." Your parents split up and your house becomes a mountain of leather and camo, a mausoleum of deer jerky. You go to your mother's on weekends but she is a hollow mess of *Gilmore Girls* and YouTube, claiming she doesn't log in or comment. Sapphire tells you her parents are divorced too. Tells you the pain is suburban and banal but no less real. You lie awake thinking of Fukushima. You lie awake doom-scrolling. You dream the burning Amazon, imagine ash and fireweed arriving on your doorstep in smiling boxes slashed with arrows. You and Sapphire and Jenna sit on the school steps on Fridays, make signs that read WRECKED CONCILIATION and THE LAST CARE. You tunnel into calculus, burrow electrochemistry thinking med school, thinking scholarship, longing to believe you might change something, there might be things you could control. You apply to universities next to the ocean, get into all of them. You do the Toxic Tour, frequent protests, lean into the snug of slogans. "Keep the oil in the soil!" Megaphones outside the fences. Ten people, twenty. "Separate oil and state!" Peaceful protest after peaceful protest until finally Sapphire says enough. She says she can't do it. She says something needs to break and there is a wild wind in her eyes and you think yes, you think of water, of the place where stone becomes sediment, where fear turns risk. You think of all the little cracks in the dam that fuse into flood.

28/06/2019. This is the work of the Oilgarchs themselves, the White Powerfuls who left us no choice. There is a term—tail gas—for the leftovers of oil refinery production. For what does not become gasoline or jet fuel or polyethylene, for what does not become

*your toothbrush, your chewing gum, the sunscreen rainbowing
from your skin.*

"THERE SHE IS." Sapphire points down Christina towards
Vidal, squat blocks of brooding plants and spires, the city
within the city. The sun blares—another heat warning today.
Lucy pulls up quiet in the Toyota pickup, a *Frozen* Thermos
in her hands. "Water has memory," she jokes as me and
Sapphire cram into the graveyard of Scratch & Win tickets
and crushed double-doubles, all of us squished in the front
of the cab.

We pass Rainbow Park, pass the Aamjiwnaang burial
ground. I look at the plant hunched on the other side it,
think down to all those bodies, buzzing hydraulic. Jenna
once told me that every city is a necropolis, built on its own
bones. Lucy pulls the top off the Thermos, flashes the black
muck, a slow coil of steam in the throat of the Thermos. In
the rear-view, a train curls into the plants, behind it the
river thrashing with sequined light. Sapphire hands me the
Ringwraith mask, slides hers on, reaches for the Thermos.

"Look," Lucy says. "I sympathize. I get you. Most of us
don't dream of valve monkeying."

"But?"

Lucy points to the rear-view mirror, the refineries. "Sure
about this?"

Sapphire thumbs her navel. Beneath it hangs the white
tear of an old piercing gone wrong. "I'm a big girl," she says.

I slip the mask on and Sapphire hands me the Thermos,
the truck rolling slow among the offices. "There he is,"
Sapphire hisses. She glares, and I follow her gaze. He's

stout, balding, trotting down the steps of the Streamline office building. Behind him, a thousand windows blare blue. He wears aviators and khakis, rummages for keys as he shuffles towards his vehicle: a grey pickup with a BABY ON BOARD bumper sticker, hockey sticks hooking out of the bed.

"Now," Sapphire urges.

"What? I thought we were both—"

"He's leaving," Sapphire hisses.

I step out of the vehicle, stand on the sidewalk in the blare of heat and asphalt. A ghost shimmers out from the truck's tailpipe, and I feel my world go light, moon-like. The cement wobbling, gooing into a swamp of liquid stone.

The target's vehicle starts. When I tap on the window, he smiles kind, sweet, shows salesman teeth. "Do it," Sapphire shouts, and a hot river sends through me as I fling my arm, release a slurp of black. For a moment I see his fear, grow giddy in the glee of it. The fear I was cradled in, that licked the wound of me. He steps on the gas and the vehicle lurches a few feet forward, then stops. The man is screaming, opening the truck door, slumping into the street.

"Oil pig," Sapphire screams. "Gas giant!" And I'm running, a tumble of fear and thrill. Jumping in the cab and laughing, panting, heart cantering. "Holy shit," Sapphire says. "You got him." She takes my shoulder, shakes it proud. The tires squeal and screech as we approach the corner. In the rear-view, he kneels in the street, hands on his face, praying to the smoke-scarred sky. The pain comes before I see it: a black tear crawling down my knuckles.

28/06/2019. On his neck, near the clavicle, he bore a hooked black scar the size of a leech. The doctors said theophylline, montelukast, beta 2-agonist. Though the fluid mostly missed the face and did not enter the eye or other sensitive areas, doctors described edema, circumferential burns, the tourniquet effect of bitumen cooled and hardened on the skin. Yesterday's incident on the front steps of the Streamline office on Vidal Street, Sarnia, was not the work of the Oilgarchs bloggers. Like tail gas, the events of today were an inevitable by-product of the Regime of Toxicity.

THOUGH THE BRAIN was not in the river, this is how you hold it in the swill of your mind—a jar nestled among the mussels, the lakeweed, the tossed needles and tires. The river is forty feet deep, more in some places, and it runs fast, all that lake squeezing into concrete watersheds, sending under its twinned tiara and down to Lake St. Clair. But the brain in the jar in the river is thoughtful, careful, waiting patient for the right solution of mercury and benzene to rust the lid just so. The perfect weft of current to tip the jar, pry its mouth and send this glob of lobe and blood vessel and grey matter floating among the crayfish and the mud puppies, the lost sunglasses and flip-flops, the walleye and smelt.

19/08/2019. The company media said the attack was random, an amateur-organized isolated incident. They were right—it was amateur. It was foolish. Everyone lives in Chemical Valley, but there are degrees. There is privilege, wealth, proximity. It can be hard to see this when you live in the throat of a dragon, but there are wrong ways to resist.

ME AND JENNA walk away from the Starbucks, cubes melting in our iced lattes. It's the first time we've seen each other since the last day of school. A pigeon hobbles through a patch of stunned grass as we approach the river's blue delirium. The twinned bands of the bridge arcing over it, trucks pulling their payloads into the U.S., the mirror city twinkling smokestacks and tail gas, smelling of money and sick.

It took a month for the hearing to happen, for the defendant to drop the charges, the judge to deem sufficient remorse. They never linked Sapphire or her cousin, though they found suspicious searches on my computer. *Online anonymity. Dark web. IP address encryption.* The target, Martin Aucoin, didn't lose his position as VP Operations. The company doubled down on their countermedia efforts. Sponsoring baseball tournaments. Saying community, reconciliation. Mr. Aucoin left the company, moved north on a severance package, decided not to press charges against the teenage girl who had shut down the blog and sent a personal apology. *Much as I wish it was*, the letter had said, *the tragedy of oil is no executive's fault. There is no Hitler to this Reich.*

Jenna asks if I'm still planning on attending the Human Knowledge Factory. I laugh and tell her yeah, thumb the burn scar on my knuckles. A truck roars past, ersatz bull testicles wagging silver on the trailer hitch. She asks where I'll go and I say somewhere next to the ocean, with good air.

We arrive at Point Edward, head towards the river's ludicrous blue, our silence soaked with Sapphire—how she hasn't apologized, how she's moved to Toronto to be with her dad, how it's all dissolving now. No other jumpers here yet so we climb over the guardrail, watch a rust-red lake freighter blare by, a pair of motorboats flanking. Overhead, the bridge catches sunlight as trucks brave the heat of August.

"When I was a girl I used to imagine it falling."

Jenna fixes on me, so I explain. Point to the bridge and tell her how I'd look at the weight of the trucks and think of the bridge's sheer implausibility. How does a thing like that become natural—ninety thousand tons of steel and asphalt hanging in the sky?

I squint up at the clouds, mine for strength. "Look," I manage. "I'm sorry. You were right."

"Always am," she shouts, twirling into a flip, landing perfect, feet-first, then gone. I follow her into the water, its perfect pollution. I changed nothing, yet I am changed. I resolved nothing yet sometimes I still feel the rush of that man on his knees. The world revolves, dissolves, and I am swimming, treading the water's cool as juggernauts climb the sky. Below, in the unseen murk, zebra mussels clump together, cling to rocks. In the mouths of those mussels, threads of cilia sway and furl, ride the swish and bob of the current, feed the river blue.

CRUELTY

MONDAY

The thing about rodents, the exterminator tells her, is that they're a lot like oil. Deepa holds the baby, staring into clouds of spray-foam insulation flung with mouse turds. Gabby reaches towards the turds and Deepa yanks her back into sidesaddle. The exterminator grins, his teeth square white suns, and repeats about mice, about oil. She has just told him about Dan, how he works in research at the Streamline plant. Something to do with catalysts. A trick an older married cousin taught her, years ago: whenever you feel the numb root of a distant want, speak your spouse's name.

She asks what he means—rodents and oil—and he twirls a flashlight, says ubiquitous, invisible. "Just like how there's pipelines all around you but you never see them." He grins. "Same thing with the rodents." He clucks, looks around the beams, the rafters, the spray-foam. "More mice in this city than people."

Deepa sniffs, looks down at Gabby—her astronaut one-sie, the grime in her wrist-rolls, the squid-shaped splotch of crimson behind her right ear. Stork's kiss.

"There are those we live with, and those that live among us." The exterminator brandishes his flashlight. Slings it among the cobwebbed beams. Deepa swallows, rights her-self, shifts the baby from hip to hip. The exterminator makes a kissy face, and Gabby laughs wetly.

Deepa swallows again. "She's just started crawling. The other day I found a pellet mushed into the heel of her hand." Deepa has been reading about hantavirus, electrical fires. Should he be wearing a mask? Should she? "Should I be concerned?"

"'Course you should," he says. "I just got back from three weeks' medical leave."

Deepa pulls the baby closer, smells her milk-sweet musk. "I was quarantined from my kids."

"Oh. From the…" She scurries her hand.

"Typhoid toxin." He nods slow, clucks. How could an exterminator have thick black hair, pale blue eyes? "Was what they determined."

He spins nimble, shining his flashlight over soccer balls and boxes of soggy textbooks. Stooping, he steps along the patchy concrete, around the grey pillars, paint slopped on. He clucks discovery. "Have a look over here." Deepa follows him to the front corner, near the laundry machine. He pulls out a stainless-steel stick that unfolds like an umbrella. The contraption has a small square mirror on the end of it, with which he taps the floor. "That's all hollow," he says, angling the mirror to see into a hole. "Been burrowed out. Likely a nest."

Deepa remembers the realtor's phrase when they bought the house last year: "Good bones." She wonders about the anatomy of houses. She's thought often about their secret passageways, their nightly travels into baseboards and over beams, through the secret worlds behind the drywall. Good bones for gnawing, for burrowing.

"I read online that you don't use poison?"

"Nope." He smugs. "Very controversial, even in the pest control community." She'd read that online too. "Do you know what it does to them?" Deepa nods. This was yesterday's Google binge. The nod doesn't stop him. "Dehydration," he says. "They shrivel up. Kidneys, liver. They drink and drink but can't absorb the fluid. Ever been thirsty? Really thirsty?"

Deepa looks down at Gabby. Pictures her child shriveled, squirming, her body seizing up as she leans over a bowl of water, drinks and drinks and drinks.

Real Gabby coos oblivious. Clucks, flails her fingers at Deepa's breast. On the way up the stairs, he points out a beam along the unfinished basement. He taps the beam with a wizened fingertip, tells her about mouse highways. Before the patio doors, he tells her about the scent trails, how the mice aren't likely to leave once they've nested. She tells him about the snap traps, the noise machines, the steel wool. She's seen them scurrying through the makeshift shelf where she keeps her pyjamas. She watched one scamper up the fibreboard, scrabble through her yoga pants. "Why would they do that? There's no food upstairs."

They pause in the doorway. "They're very resourceful," he says. "They learn, adapt." He looks at her, takes her in.

Her body glows. She senses the skim of clothes against her skin. "Do you think a cat would help?"

"Oh yeah," he says.

"Well," she says. "Unfortunately, my husband."

The exterminator grins. "Yes," he says. "Unfortunate."

Dan developed asthma a few years after starting at the plants, where both his parents had worked all their lives. Once they visited a friend who had two obese orange tomcats and Dan had coughed all night, stumbled to the walk-in clinic at 8:00 a.m. to get a prescription for a puffer.

The exterminator goes outside, measures the ground with a wheeled stick. He takes pictures, writes on a clipboard. She puts the baby in the activity centre, watches Gabby swat the plastic monkey, pull on Big Bird until he croaks the alphabet song. He comes back inside with a yellow requisition form. A number at the bottom. A nauseating number. Close to two thousand dollars.

"Fairly large procedure," he explains. He thumbs his collar as he describes the series of screens they'll put in, the holes they'll plug. He mentions sealants, trenches, foundation vents. "We'll need to open up your deck," he explains. "There's parts of your basement I could stick my arm right through and shake your hand." He mimes it, flattening his fingers, then jabbing through the house of her. Handing her his business card, he says he's not one to brag but he's good at what he does. He taps the card, its gloss, its lush. At the top there's the company logo—a grinning cartoon rat—and his name: *Pierce Trembley, Owner Operator*. Below: *All work 100% guaranteed for life*.

He puts a hand on hers. "Trust me," he says. "You're doing the right thing."

She holds the yellow estimate as she watches him climb into his van. The yellow van has a six-foot black plastic tail spiraling up from the back bumper, a pair of cartoony mouse ears swinging off the front of the roof. On the back doors, a smiling cartoon rat next to the company name: *Simply the Pest: Cruelty Free Pest Control*. Watching the van swagger off the curb, she wonders not if he can solve her problem—she is not that foolish—but whether he can help her find it, feed it, map its bones.

FIVE MONTHS EARLIER, the day after they'd closed on the house, Deepa had cleaned some leaves off the back stairs and found a pile of raccoon dung. The deck boards were reeking and rotten. She raked off the scat, borrowed a pressure washer, put down vinegar. The next day she found new droppings. Runged black slugs clotted with berry seeds. "Almost looks like crude," Dan had said. It was because of the pond, the neighbour told her, bouncing the baby in September sun. A lithe woman, her scalp extravagant with grey. She meant the long-neglected pond the house had come with. "Attracts all kinds of rodents." Flinging a beaming Gabby to "The Grand Old Duke of York," she said: "You could always try Ex-Lax. I've heard it works miracles—depending how you feel about animal cruelty." Deepa took the baby back, trying not to snatch.

They had not used Ex-Lax. They'd drained the pond and cleaned the shit. But the phrase still swam the sleep-starved river of Deepa's mind.

That night was the first time she'd heard them. Listening to the baby cry, willing her to sink back down and subdue, Deepa heard the walls come alive with chew-claw nocturnes. Scritching, scritching. The next morning she changed the baby's diaper without cleaning the high chair mess, returned to find a grey lump shooting for the corner, slinking into some unseen crevice. Once she was attuned, she discovered them everywhere. Rattles in the stove, under the sink. Cruelty. Trails of poo, small black nuggets along the baseboards, jewelled into the hardwood, smooshed into her child's knees. Animal. She flipped over the bath mat: a scatter of dung. She stalked her home on all fours, inspecting black fragments. Took her glasses off to squint. Pocket lint, blackberry chunk, toast crumb. Turd. She dreamt herself wading through oceans of dung. Cruelty. Her life became kneeling over the carpet picking up tiny black ovals. Fearfully plucking tufts out of Dan's whiskers. Dan had laughed, or shrugged. He never picked up a turd. When she'd bought the snap traps he'd flinched and let the spring shoot the steel back, almost snatching his finger. "Jesus," he'd said. "Can we put these in paper bags? I don't want to touch one." One Wednesday the baby pulled herself onto the coffee table, staring cross-eyed into her hand, two flattened black nuggets at the base of her palm. She brought them closer, mouth open, starting to drool. Deepa had leapt and tackled her child, put the exterminator on speakerphone as she ran hot water and scrubbed her child's hands raw.

HER PROBLEM IS the open secret, her daily torture, this milksuck monotony. Her problem is a mind full of IKEA high chairs, of Astroturf bottle-drying racks, of the relative merits of footed pyjamas. Reading *Goodnight Moon* for two hundred days straight. Oaty Chomps, fruit packs, a kitchen flung wild with drinkable yogurt. Her problem is diapers, diaper rash, Diaper Genies, diaper blowouts, diaper shame, plastic diaper guilt, the non-existence of biodegradable diapers. Her problem is zinc cream and APNO and formula shame and hat shame and sunscreen shame and a woman in Starbucks telling her the baby must be dehydrated and she would know. "Grandmother of six." Her problem is sanitizing bottles, boiling puree. Her problem is sleep— needing a lot, going to bed by ten her whole life then entering a world of sleep regressions, sleep training, spread-sheeting the hours between naps. Her problem is growing up enraged by A-minuses, growing up braces and volleyball and scholarships to OCAD, going to the right teacher's college and getting the right limited-term appointment and then the right job teaching art at the school within walking distance, watching Dan play This Little Piggy with his nieces and thinking yeah, sure, why not. Because people say mat leave is intense but so worth it. Because men think it's a break. Because no one tells you you have trained all your life to become a full-time janitor slash wet nurse slash dragging the activity centre into the bathroom to sneak a shower. Her problem is through all this: mice. Mice crawling through the basement of her sleepless harried mind. Mice trawling every crevice of her life and Gabby hunting mouse turds and Dan insisting it's just one mouse. Dan saying why didn't she try painting, maybe a new palette, and her standing in the too-hot loft staring at the easel while Dan gloats off to work in the morning and of course the baby begins to cry and she is thinking yes, she could paint the walls of her prison but what she wants is to fray the fringe of her world, to believe that a fuck might split some seam in the shale of her.

DAN FLINGS GRINNING Gabby into the air. He suggests stir-fry, boils rice while she puts the baby down. The proud hero, the joyous fun dad home from his day's work. On the way upstairs, she finds three fresh turds. Rounding the corner next to the laundry hamper, she sees a thumb-sized mouse wheel and scamper into the baseboard. She screams at it, flails a foot and stomps. Gabby stares at her, shocked out of her drowse. Deepa hums on desperate, her arms quivering. *Down will come baby.* It takes all of her not to shriek. *Cradle and all.*

Back downstairs she gazes into the grainy wonderland of the monitor and tells Dan she's on the edge, is worried about what she might do. "Trust me," Dan says, looking into the rice he's boiling, "I hate the mouse too. But we can't afford that estimate."

Dan insists on calling it "the mouse" in his minimizing tone though Deepa knows that if you see one you have a hundred. She knows their shit is toxic. She knows the thick membrane between sanity and desperation.

Dan goes to work. He leaves. He does not spend the brief jewel of naptime crawling around on all fours with a Kleenex, foraging for turds.

"Wait," Dan says, fluffing the rice, squinting. "The thing about his quarantine, the typhoid. Was that the first thing he said?"

"No. Why?"

Dan laughs, stops himself. "It's just. I wonder if he just says that every time he sees someone with a kid." He chuckles. "Pretty smart, actually." Dan plates the rice, pulls the lid off the wok. "Call someone else tomorrow? A second opinion?"

"Sure."

After dinner they go upstairs and watch three-quarters of an episode of *Greenleaf* and turn off the lights. Dan reaches for her hip and she shivers into herself, says sorry, not tonight, she's exhausted. He nods, wilts into his pillow. Some nights he takes his iPhone to the bathroom and she pretends not to notice when he comes back flushed, drained. Deepa is not jealous of his private browsing window. She's thankful that it spares her. She would trade a lifetime of sex for thirty minutes of sleep.

But it comes to Dan, not her. She thinks of mice, of highways of them. She listens for the snap traps and the baby and the sounds in the walls while Dan tumbles into snore. She finds herself thinking of Pierce, holding the glow of him, wondering what he smells like, how clean he keeps his van. The baby starts to grunt. Then whimper. *Fuck you*, Deepa thinks to the baby as she stirs awake. *Fuck you*. Then, *I'm sorry*. Then, *I love you but please not yet*.

TUESDAY

She dreams the mouse highway, a mouse gas station, pipeline filled with scurrying rodents. Mice crammed, scrambling over each other, shoulder to shoulder, tail to nose. flighty, pink-footed, squeaking, the soundless rush of their tiny legs. Furred blobs race in the pipeline, heedless of ceiling or wall, their biomass sending through the underland. On the surface, feet and tires click and drag their daily oblivion of chores but here the slurp of fur and flesh grows whiskered faces, faces that flash tiny beaming teeth, astonishing and white.

DEEPA IS LAYING bananas on the conveyor when she spots him at the self-checkout. His green-grey coveralls, a company windbreaker, his salt-and-pepper hair. Deepa presents her points card and taps her credit card as she watches the exterminator put his pin into the machine. He buys a smoothie and a package of sushi. He does not take a receipt. She bags her yogurt, muesli, and bananas slowly, making time for the encounter. For a moment it seems like he'll walk out the other way. She focuses on the baby, wiggles the strap of her black bag. Gabby snorts and grabs for it.

He turns, then. Walks towards her, passing the auction art.

"Pierce," she says, half to herself.

He sees her, then, and smiles. The cool white dazzle of his teeth. Approaching, he stoops to make goofy fingers for the baby. She notes the label on his sushi: *vegetarian California roll*.

"Your place is pretty close, right. Can I walk you? I like a stroll at lunch."

She shrugs like sure, checking the baby's diaper while her heart thumps and flutters. He sips his green smoothie while she adjusts Gabby's onesie and toque. Then they walk together through the automated doors. In the parking lot, knowing it's ridiculous, she scans for watching eyes. The want throbs through her, thick and secret. How could others not detect it?

Deepa pushes the baby up the grey streets, leaves circling in the wind, and asks how one gets into the extermination profession. He mock-shudders. "*Humane* pest control." Then he explains how he worked for a poison-using company for five months before he even thought seriously about the death. He says it happened gradually: first he started imagining their bodies filling an oil drum, then an entire dumpster. He imagined them rotting everywhere he went. Saw heaps of them. He dreamt, once, of an entire ocean of mouse bodies, ebbing and flowing gently against a pristine white-sand beach.

He swallows hard. Watching the ball of his throat, she thinks of snakes digesting rodents. They turn onto her street and he tells her how he's been to all sorts of places, from average homes like hers to the grimiest walk-ups. He's even been through a few of the mansions in town, Streamline execs and bank bigwigs. The owner of the Sarnia Sting. "Mice don't differentiate," he says. "They don't smell wealth."

"Wow." She chuckles. "The great democratizer."

"That's just it." He smiles. "Everybody's got pests."

"And most of us want to kill them."

He doesn't smile. "Listen," he says, as they approach her house. "I can get you a better price. Which would mean visits. Several." His blue eyes wince, tidal, as he comes closer, smelling of salt and want. She feels the press of him, his day's-work heft. She is a blade of grass, tingling in a breeze.

Gabby reaches up from her stroller. "Bah," she says, grinning, pointing to the house. She has Dan's unibrow, his swamp-water eyes.

Deepa touches Pierce's chest, sends him gently backwards. "I can't—I just—I need—I should get her inside." She is pleading with herself.

He grins. That star-white smile. "Think about it," he says.

BACK AT HOME, Deepa reads an article about mall mice. Turns out the Yorkdale mall is infested with them. The article is by a woman who worked at the H&M and sometimes when they had to watch the security camera they'd see hordes of them racing out green-eyed in the glitching UV dark. Deepa closes her eyes and rests in the orbit of this image. The lime-washed world of the night-vision camera as the mall shuts down, the lights go off, and the legion mice emerge. Thousands of them—grey and white and brown, quick as wind. Scurrying through the hallways, climbing on the benches, pausing to sniff and munch, cruising over the counters, tails bouncing and licking in their wake. She imagines herself strapped to the mall floor, unable to move, the mice creeping over her like a twitching, many-nosed blanket.

After snack and diaper change and the naptime routine, Deepa looks the exterminator up on Facebook. Pierce Tremblay. She finds that his account is public. Gabby puts blocks into her mouth as Deepa stares at pictures of the exterminator in a sou'wester and waist-high yellow boots. Pictures of him in a pine forest on the back of a snowmobile, the conifers sighing with white. Pictures of him holding three grinning children in Halloween costumes—two Elsas and a slashed-pillowcase phantom. She notes that there are no pictures of him in quarantine, but why would there be? Most of the photos are flattering. Perhaps he filters them.

She lies on the couch and submits to a thin, dusty sleep. She hears scratching in the walls. Sounds that could be the finger-play of trees on kitchen windows. She dreams the baby as a mouse-thing in a diaper, the pale blue cloth one she uses in the mornings. Fat baby cheeks and buttocks, long gnarl of a tail, human hands, a patch of brown in her white coat. The baby mouse stops at every turd. Inspects each pellet cross-eyed, the way Gabby examines new foods. Soon small black ovals are clinging to her knuckles, fingers, the heels of her hands. The mouse-child stops, sits, brings the turds closer, tail flicking with pleasure. Deepa wants to yell, to scream. Even gets her mouth open, but the sound simply wobbles, caught in the gelatine walls of her dream. Then the exterminator is there, scooping up the child. He is wearing yellow boots over his coveralls, and has grown taller, squarer. His nose is longer, framed by cartoon whiskers. He holds his mouse-girl in an open palm, deftly flicks each clod away. Then turns to the child and strokes her, tenderly, with one long finger. The baby shivers with joy. Dream-Deepa steps forward. Finds herself moving, now, with ease. She pecks her mouse-child behind the ears, thumbs the breastbone of her whiskered lover. The three of them lie down on a crimson divan, coiling into each other, breathing, touching, listing.

LUCY CALLS THE THEORY "Sexual Animal Avatar." The premise is that everyone makes love like an animal. Her husband, she explains, is an eagle on his good days, a hummingbird on his bad ones. Lucy's one-year-old Roger waddles the fuchsia sunset of the Wayfair rug, mayhems around Gabby's activity centre, smacking Big Bird. Deepa sips afternoon Pinot Grigio and says that Dan is like a beaver, maybe a penguin. "He's a bit flippery." Lucy laughs, asks her to expand, so Deepa tells about the vagina physio, the relief of not having sex, how the physio person told her she had a lot of tension in her buttocks and she couldn't explain she was holding in a fart.

Lucy cracks up. "It'll pass," she says. "Sex will be good again."

Deepa clucks, skeptical, watches Gabby roll across the monitor.

They talk about pyjamas and the Old Navy sale until she sees a brown flash streak through the kitchen, stands up rage-stamping, sees Lucy looking at her strange. Deepa exhales and tells Lucy about the naptimes she spends crawling around the carpet picking up mouse turds like some deranged platoon sergeant. She tells Lucy she's not happy and she feels terrible, feels guilt from all the blissed-out moms on her Instagram. Lucy tells her that's all normal.

"I hated work the last few months," Deepa says. "But now I miss it. I miss the crop tops, the boys reeking of BO and pot and Pizza Pizza."

Roger makes a run for Dan's banjo, grabs the neck. Deepa rushes to save it, clutching the fretboard and snapping her knuckles against the skin. She sets the banjo back, teetering, on the stand, and blurts about the exterminator. She can see Lucy trying not to laugh as Deepa says seriously, a very good-looking and apparently eager exterminator.

Lucy sips her tea and snorts. Deepa tells her no, of course she wouldn't actually do anything, but it still feels wrong. "Emotional infidelity."

"A sexy exterminator?" They're both giggling. Lucy does eyebrows: "I bet he knows his way around a cavity."

Roger creeps back towards the banjo.

"I'm serious," Deepa says. "It's serious. It's bad."

Lucy looks at her, a little stern. "Where's it coming from?" Deepa stares at the Wayfair carpet, the IKEA lamp, the Diaper Genie. She says she feels trapped and she knows this isn't the way out, knows there is no way out but she feels like she wants to shatter some wall, like breaking some picket in this fence of normal.

"It'll pass," Lucy says.

"Also I want to punish Dan, though I have no idea why."

"Talk to him," Lucy says as the banjo clangs onto the rug, a mess of twanging strings and shivering snare.

DEEPA HAD BEEN a woman who'd wanted children vaguely, who'd never thought too much about it. A woman who, once pregnant, had had to filter her social media feeds because she felt guilty and selfish reading articles about future storms, about giant carbon-sucking machines, about the animal livestock industry. A woman who didn't love newborns but who'd always seen herself as a someday mother. A woman who had once been an aspiring painter who had dated a lean science-smitten volleyball player. Who had left that boy for undergrad then teacher's college but always stayed in touch. Who came home for a job, for her family, who opened a door one day to find Dan holding a thatch of white roses, presenting a matchbox filled with cattail fluff and old man's beard and a note that said, *Tired of Tinder?* A woman who paid her union dues and nodded through PD sessions and saved money for a down payment and moved in with the man who was now a Streamline chemist with a stellar pension. So she wiped the peanut butter from his face in the morning, ordered shoes online for his mega-arched feet, pulled the trophy blackhead from his left cheek. She became a woman who did the country wedding at the family dairy farm, who laughed off the baby shower jokes, who did the honeymoon in Costa Rica and went full-time permanent and talked about it and talked about it and watched Dan throw his six-month-old nephew in the air and sink into bed with a hand on her stomach saying, "That's where the baby goes." She went off birth control expecting it to take a year, maybe more, but never got her period. She took the folic acid and did the prenatal yoga and bought the Diaper Genie. When the baby came, and robbed her of sleep, of strength and sanity, she felt a dizzying betrayal. This covenant of smiling mothers. Those mothers who had not said colic, who had not said witching hour. "It's horrible," she told everyone she could. "My baby turns into a demon," she'd told her mother-in-law, who'd looked back, breathed in, scandalized. Said, "That's the baby blues talking."

THE BABY IS STILL napping when Deepa twitches awake to a sound from behind the stove. She rises, tiptoes over. Turns on the iPhone flashlight and peers into the crevice but sees nothing. They are in there, even now. Always listening.

Then she hears it again. Tiny feet in the stove's spine. And again. Scritch. Scrabble. Hard to say how many. And then she's squatting, arms wide, hands on the side of the stove. Squatting and rocking it, wiggling the stove loose. Her back a red misery, the stove inching, creaking, inching, at last out far enough that she can look down and retch. Had she always known what she would find there? A thousand shrapnelled pellets, a million. Tufts of carpet fur, dragged doorway leaves, shredded baseboard. *A nest.* She thinks of tiny mice in frantic copulation. Looking at the back of the stove, her stomach sours. Pellets crushed and crusted into the metal. The wires gnawed and piss-stained, turds in every seam of the aluminum backplate and halfway up a grey thumb-sized tuft, a patch of dryer lint threaded with thin yellow bones, a grill of tiny grinning teeth.

POURING MALBEC into a glass, Dan tells her about his work friend who had an infestation, paid a couple hundred dollars and solved the problem with poison. "It really shouldn't cost two grand." He swirls the twelve-dollar wine and sniffs.

She says no. No poison. She rises and gets the rectangular glue traps from the cupboard, wags them like oversized bills. "I'm putting some down tonight."

"Aren't they awful? They break their legs trying to get off."

"You drop them in a bucket of water. I googled it."

He shudders, scans the floor. "With poison, they die outside. No mess."

"What if they track it? Gabby's crawling around."

"I'll plug some more holes this weekend."

Last week Dan "plugged" the gap between the counter and the fridge with steel wool, then peacocked around putting the tools away. "That should take care of it," he'd boasted. That night, she'd watched a small mouse lurch and scramble up the silvery thatch. The mouse had stared at her as it climbed, cautious and bumble-footed but seemingly unafraid. By the time she'd reached for something to whack it with, it was gone.

In bed, she notices Dan's ears. Has he gotten a haircut? She's always known they were large but tonight they are elephantine.

They eat a frozen pizza and watch thirty minutes of *Fleabag* and then they lie down to fall asleep. She lies there listening to Dan's snores. Rises, compelled by a sound. She squats naked on the hardwood, nude in yellow gloves, riffling through the cupboards. She goes through the oats and the cereals and the pasta. Nothing nothing nothing. Finally she finds a forgotten bag of rice in a low cupboard, much of it spilled. A torn bottom corner, a Stonehenge of droppings. She lifts it triumphant, sends a fountain of grains scattering over the floor. Dan appears on the stairs, looks at her with quiet disapproval as she lays down the sticky traps—stove, radiator, basement.

"What?"

"I'm worried about you."

"I'm just—I can't stand it."

"You're paranoid."

"You're useless, Dan. They're in our *home*."

"Deepa—"

"What?"

"It's just. What's this really about?"

Deepa just smiles back.

WEDNESDAY

She dreams huge vats full of turds. Black pellets heated, ventilated, cracked and catalyzed. Turds breaking down reluctantly. Great iron tubs full of black swampy liquid. In the dream she stares at the bubbling sable, wondering where it is going, where it will end up. In the distance there's a train tunnel in the side of a mountain, a shiny black vessel honking into it. Then she is holding a pole and standing on a ferry in the middle of the black lake. Holding a punting pole and trying to push but simply stirring the goop. Stirring it and looking down to see a tiny row of teeth.

IN THE MORNING Dan asks if she's all right, if they're all right. She says sure, yes, fine. He smiles angry, pours coffee into his travel mug. "Whatever that means." Once he's gone, she goes into the bathroom and realizes she didn't drain the bath last night, finds herself standing transfixed before the floating toys. They often leave the water in, so she's seen this many times before but it has never struck her. A plastic cow floats face down, angled at a slight tweak. Its tail in the air, the black-and-white girth surrounded by a scummy rime of soap. She reaches in, turning her face away as she pulls the plug.

She takes Gabby for a walk. It's a mild day. Chance of rain later. She heads towards the park on Christina, plops Gabby in one of the swings. Gabby turns, screaming giddy, when a train rumbles into the Streamline plant. Deepa tells her that's where Daddy works. On the way home, the air raid siren sounds. The World War II relic that sounds every day at 12:30. The sirens are intended as a comfort, she supposes, a protection. They are there to warn the people of Sarnia if and when there's a leak from the plants. And so they are tested every day. Some days the testing makes Deepa feel safe, watched over. Most days she doesn't think about the sound at all. But once in a while, on days like today, she feels a new sharpness in the air passing through her lungs. A faint ammoniac bite and of course it can't be real, of course she's imagining it. But she wonders about the baby. How long would it take, if the alarm sounded, if the levels were off, if there were even the slightest leak.

She changes diapers. She pulls up his contact and lets her thumb hover over the green button. She holds the estimate against her nose, her lips. She reads online about vinegar, peppermint, ammonia. How you can deter them with smell, cover over their scent trails. She lays down towels covered in peppermint. She pulls the stove out again. More shit. She clogs hole after hole with copper wire. She finds turds behind the bookcases, along the baseboards, under the couch. "It's getting colder now," her father says on the phone. "They move in. Have you considered a cat?" She answers that Dan is allergic. "Okay," her father says. "I've got to go." Deepa used to chat on the phone with her mother until her tea went cold in her hand. The house sings peppermint.

Deepa falls asleep during naptime, wakes to a squeak like school hallway sneakers. A sustained *pince*, not loud but wretched, shrill. She hits the volume button on the monitor, sees Gabby face down in her sleep sack. The raised potato of her diapered bum.

She opens the door and sees them quivering. Four grape-sized babies skittering on the basement stairs. Tiny legs scrabbling, clawing. Overlong feet. Days old at most, pink skin blooming grey. All their muscles shuddering. Tails flicking back and forth, back and forth.

She gets the yellow gloves and works them on. Then she picks up the glue trap and lowers it slowly over them, plucking them up one by one. They vibrate awfully as she walks outside, sinks both gloved hands deep in the bucket, holds her breath until the movement stops.

Once it's in the garbage bag, in the outside trash can, she phones.

A SMALL, LIGHTLY FURRED creature with bilateral symmetry. The Himalayan salt lamp. Fruit pouches contain none of the fibre, just fructose boiled into textureless goop. Common predators include owls, foxes, lizards, and snakes. The house mouse communicates through pheromones, particularly those excreted through their urine. The mouse's whiskers allow it to detect air movement and surfaces. Recent testing on mice has determined that, as with human infants, the ultrasonic cries of mouse pups stimulates the production of the "love hormone" oxytocin in mothers. Dan saying, "I think she's hungry." Upon hearing the cries of their pups, mouse mothers hurry back to their children and carry them to the safety of their nest.

SHE RESTS HER FOREHEAD on Pierce's chest, grinds it up to meet his eyes. He is panting, flushed. Part of her had wished he would scurry, make love like a rodent. But he was slow, poised. He checked in often and seemed to be trying not to rush it, trying to cling to the moment as it melted into memory. She remembers a phrase Lucy said once: "Spank-bank eyes."

She goes to the bathroom and sits there in the husk of some desolate city, vehicles gone to rust in the middle of streets. She sees, as if in a time-lapse, the mice emerge. Hordes of them crawling over the ruins. Mice swarming grey over the concrete, scrambling triumphant over curbs, washing over street and sidewalk. Tiny bodies fast and chattering, their fur the colour of concrete, of stone. She sees herself there, too. Her body cast in stone, lying in the middle of the street. Her mouth is open and the mice are crawling over her neck, up her chin, scrambling over her ears, bouncing shoulders to cram into her throat.

She doesn't hear it, doesn't need to. Somewhere, her baby is crying. She opens the bathroom door to find Pierce lying in their nest of blankets, a Canada flag tattoo gone pale and warped on his chest. On the monitor, Gabby is whining, her hands on the white bars of her crib.

"You need to go," Deepa says.

He nods, pats the floor for his coveralls. "I'll text you," he says, stepping towards her like a kiss goodbye.

She dekes him because she already knows what she always has known: that she is both mouse and exterminator, that there is no house without pests. Upstairs, she opens the blackout blinds. Bares the city, the houses, the plants.

Somewhere, vats churn and rush with boiling bitumen. Somewhere, molecules catalyze. Somewhere, mice make nests, sneak homes.

She stands next to the crib in sacred darkness and takes up her child. Puts her hand on her child's back and feels the rhythm of her breath. Then she reaches in, takes Gabby in her arms. Her child, kicking groggily in her sleep sack. Snorting, smiling. She hears the front door open, sees Dan half run up the stairs, pause halfway. She steps onto the landing and tells him she couldn't, she needed to, they were babies, sweet dying helpless babies with no mother and no food. "You should have seen them. Starving. Shivering."

He's closer now, holding something. A shoebox. He grins his dopey grin, front teeth peeking through. He opens the lid and she sees the grey and black stripes, the milky green eyes. Gabby squeals, leans forward, sends a hand towards it. The kitten scratches lazily against the side of her box, ringed tail flicking, eyes pert. Dan says he got her from work, one of the operators had a litter. "They've been calling her Six," he says. "Because of the paw."

He nods down, and Deepa sees the extra toe on the front left foot. As she reaches down to stroke that limb the cat bends into her hand, licks her finger with a tiny coarse tongue. Then she goes for the drawstring of Deepa's hoodie. Bats it and leaps out of the shoe box, begins to crawl up Deepa's arm, tail licking and curling.

The cat comes face to face with Gabby. Sniffs her. Licks the air.

"She's perfect," Deepa says, holding the cat in one arm, the baby in the other. "Your allergies?"

Dan reaches into his breast pocket, produces a box of Reactine. He says he did some reading, that it turns out you can get used to your own cat's dander after a while. The symptoms don't go away, but they lessen.

"What should we call her?"

Deepa gazes into her yellow-flecked eyes, and knows. "Hunter." She steps towards Dan. Squeezes the baby between the two of them, juggles the circling clawing cat. The afternoon light slants pale over the room as she holds them—her husband, her hunter, her child. Dan pushes his nose into the side of her neck and she feels his big lower lip, the smooth patch in his stubble, the slight cork in his chin. The smell of his sandalwood shaving cream.

She remembers him, then. Remembers the man who learned Appalachian-style banjo, who wrote a comic song about the time she cried over a cheese gone to mould. The man who came back from visiting his nephew and put a hand on her stomach and said, "That's where the baby goes." The man who twirled her shameless on the waterfront, refinery lights dancing in the river, a slurred cosmos. The man who'd held their child in the red wash of his headlamp and rubbed his fingers in her wounded mouth after the laser surgery because, yes, that was a form of love. A man who'd bought *The Birth Partner* and offered to massage her perineum. The man who'd refused to sleep during her labour, who'd packed a bag with chocolate and diced mango and a Walmart housecoat. Who'd fed her Popsicles and stood behind her for thirty-six hours whispering "low tones" and "you're doing great" and even when she'd hissed to stop touching her she couldn't stand it he'd stood a few feet away and said, "I'm here, I'll be just over here."

That night she lies awake knowing she will tell Dan, will hurt him. Knowing there is no way to explain. Knowing it could take years. She imagines the weight of them in the garbage bag. The clear kind Dan buys. Next to the tin foil, the tight-rolled diapers, the green label: *Catchmaster*. The bag stretched weepy around the curled corners of the trap. She feels the weight of the baby mice, their grey thimble bodies. And she sees that she was, of course, the mouse all along. The secret, subterranean thing, burrowing frantic, seeking some nourishment, some lull to a pain small and private and fiercely real. That she has both lost herself and culled her kin. Beside her, Dan snores gentle, a hitch in his inhale. Hunter slinks onto the bed, paws her face, purrs her into narcotic slumber. She feels a pipeline inside her. Something pulped and pouring within. Not an end of hurt, but a movement of it. A flow. Dead grey babies cling to a glue trap and she would like to think their rot a genesis, a making of wane.

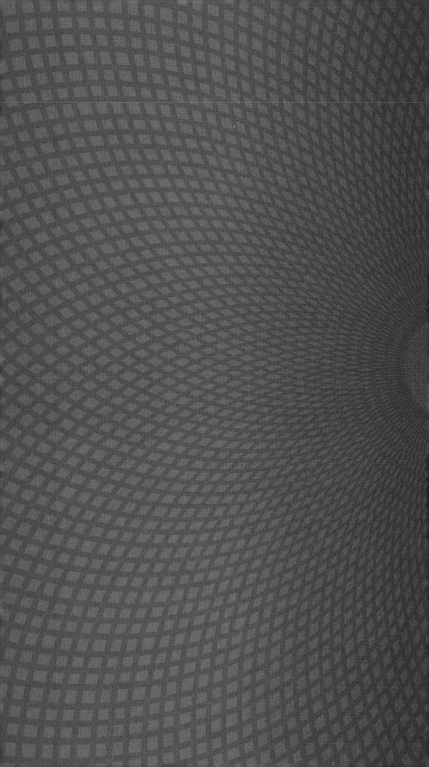

Dream
Haven

SIX SIX
TWO FIFTY

THERE'S A TAP on my shoulder and Coach tells me I'm up.
I ask who but he just nods out towards the ice where Scab
Benoit's lining up on the left wing. So I hop the boards,
skate out into the crowd's feral purr. Scab opens his bust-
ed-picket-fence mouth into a grin and wiggles his mitts as
if we needed a signal. Eyeing his teeth, I ask if he'll get
some implants with this year's PIM bonus and he starts
beaking faster than a hungry seagull. Starts saying I'm
dragging knees, saying I've got a stride like a lame jack-
rabbit and do I need to borrow some tape for my ankles. I
tell him to cool his jet stream, tell him to wait until Stripes
drops the biscuit before I shatter his jaw. Scab says something about the snatch of the sister I don't have and the ref
drops the puck and we're tossing mitts and cocking elbows
and squaring up in the bright white open.

The arena a seashell, conjuring oceans. The strange hissing emptiness of twenty thousand screams.

"I fight guys like you on my way to real fights. Just fucking saying."

Scab keeps his fists close but I can see they're yellow and bloated from his scrap last night in Buffalo. He's taking his time so I unclip my helmet and nod it off. Then I tell him he'd be wise to keep his bucket on for this one. When he reaches for his chinstrap I clutch his sweater and whale, clap his jaw once, twice, glance his helmet on the third swing.

The crowd whistling and shrieking and my heart pattering wild. That glow in my fist meaning pain later and strength now and Scab still standing, breathing hard.

"You're a fuckin' jizzrag," Scab yells over the crowd and then he fakes one and lands one, opens the old wound above my left eye. Quicker than I remembered. Scab keeps swinging and swinging and it's all I can do to grab his sweater and hold him off with a stiff-arm and thank fuck I have reach on him because my socket is fast filling with hot bright darkness.

That stun ended by another: Scab's fist clacking my chin. Half the world red and missing as Scab keeps hammering, the refs closing in to stop it. I tug him in and turn my face away and we both land a few more body shots and then I drop, yank him down to the ice, pull him close and hold him there.

The sweet cool balm of the ice under me while the crowd howls above. Scab's body curls into mine and the heave of our lungs gradually merges. We hold each other, breathing in sync. A drool of my blood leaks down onto the white of his sweater. The lovely warm clarity of it.

"Good fight." Scab pants, and I tell him: "Same."

I'M SITTING AT THE BAR with a beer and a bourbon and my right fist stuffed in a wine chiller, the ice melted into salty gazpacho. Three new stitches in the braid of scars along my left eyebrow and according to the team doctor I can't fight for a month. Not fighting for a month meaning four weeks as a healthy scratch and the live possibility of getting traded or sent down to ride the bus.

The place is dry even for a Tuesday and Sudsy and Moose have already ghosted home to their wives. Smithy and Taylor are the only others left and they keep stacking rounds of Patrón in front of me, rounds of Patrón I pour into the wine chiller when they're not looking. Smithy and Taylor calling me a beauty, saying how that scrap was so ferda and they'd pull the fire alarm if I dropped the mitts and there's nothing better than a man bleeding for his team.

I know they mean it but I also know I'll never score a pro goal and they'll never fight on my behalf and I'll likely retire with five career points and CTE. Two cup rings and zero recorded playoff minutes and I'd have to be pretty dull not to realize that I'm the guy who takes punches for the guys who score goals. A fighter on a team of hockey players.

Smithy and Taylor tell me I'm a fuckin' beautician and I nod and grin and dump another tequila into the chiller and find myself hunching over my phone, searching for Tinderella. Find myself turning into Mr. Swipes Right. I get a reply from a girl named Stacey who has a pug licking her neck in her profile pic which I guess is meant to show her sweet side. Stace tells me she's tired of the bar scene and I tell her I'm tired of dominating the bar scene and she sends me a Noah's ark of emojis and then I'm popping a Cialis and climbing into my truck and heading for the Loop, city lights slurring through the dark.

SUITING UP FOR practice Smithy and Taylor are asking me where I skedaddled to last night. "Slay the dragon, Sudsy?" "Hit the clinic this morning?" "The slipper fit?" It's all chuckles and high fives and backcheck forecheck paycheque as we head out towards the ice but then Coach pulls me aside and asks if I saw what Taylor was tweeting last night. Coach wiggles his rat-grey moustache, bald scalp glowing womb-pink under the rink lights, and asks if I saw my mug all over the *Tribune* website, a dozen empty shot glasses twinkling on the bar. I tell him no but I can imagine and he says you better smarten up unless you want to head down to Rockford. Says he likes me and I'm a good dressing room guy but I'm a lot easier to replace than Smithy or Taylor and I tell him yes coach because I'm not eager to sell my house and move to the fifth new city in ten years.

Coach doesn't care that I played regular minutes for five years in div one, that I led my team's defencemen in points for two of those five years. Doesn't care that I was the only student athlete at Penn State to graduate magna cum laude in kinesiology and he seriously doesn't care that I anchored the power play on a major midget team that won the Ontario provincial championship. Coach genuinely doesn't know that I have a harder clapper than half our d-men, doesn't care that I have an ex-wife and a little girl. Coach has won two cups in the past five years which means he is not obliged to care that most of the league is moving away from keeping pure fighters. To him I am a giant fist with skates on. Yes, Coach gives me the odd pity shift as a seventh defenceman when we're up a few but he still clearly thinks my only real skill is knuckling jaw. Thinks and is not scared to vocalize that there are plenty of guys in the league who will punch face without complaining or causing media shenanigans or asking for ice time.

It gets hard thinking of yourself as a hockey player when you get one non-fighting shift every five or six games, which is why I like practice. Shooting pucks at pro goalies who know I can snipe my portion. I get a sweat going and gradually forget about Stacey and Coach and just get into the rhythm of active sticks and hard strides and crisp passes. The boys chirping me about pizzas, calling me apple turnover. Coach hollering his mantra: "It's all about economy of motion." Yelling "economy of motion" over and over until I start hearing it as a story about a girl named Connie Demotion, a girl I have to dig deeper and deeper to resist.

WHAT HAPPENED WITH STACEY was she mentioned something raunchy, something dark. Something I wasn't expecting from a soft-faced nurse who'd admitted she'd been watching *Gilmore Girls* when I messaged her. I told her I don't do this particular dark kink and asked why she didn't mention this before I was in her living room with my bare feet on her zebra-print rug. She said it wasn't a big deal, said she was still up for whatever and then I saw this look in her eyes like

Rebecca used to have when she wanted more from me but didn't have it in her to ask. Then Stacey's pug, Gorgonzola, came over and I started rubbing it around the neck and I guess the gorgon got really excited because his eyeball jumped out. His eyeball scooted straight out of its socket. Not like I saw the little tendrils connecting it to the brain or anything but it just sort of deked out in a way that was clearly not right, perched at the cusp of the skull like an orange held in a mouth.

Stacey was not concerned. She said he'd had three surgeries and there was nothing she could really do so she leaned down and pulled his eyelids out and over the ball and then just popped it back in with her thumb. Which how could someone not find that hilarious? Stacey popping her pug's eyeball straight back into its socket and the dog sitting there panting and snorting and breathing louder than a snoozing bear and all of it was too awful so I shot back on the couch laughing. Stacey got into it too and soon we were both cackling. Sitting there wheezing in a condo on the thirtieth floor, looking out over the river and the city lights, a belligerent hard-on going numb in my pants.

WHEN YOU'RE six six two fifty everyone in the league wants to fight you. When you're this size guys can make a name for themselves by landing a knuckle in your personal space. Dusters become fan favourites in a slick instant, even if all they do is hug and block and throw little body jabs that couldn't bruise a rib. The other thing that happens when it's your job to hurt people in front of twenty thousand spectators is that people notice. People watch. People record and tweet and blog. Joe Nobodies come on Twitter and beak off about how you're a skeezbag because you ran their team's goalie and can you really write back that you were just doing exactly what your coach told you to, exactly what you get paid for, exactly what someone else will do if you decide to turn your hairy nose up? When you make your living throwing punches, sometimes you get heated. Sometimes you tell someone that if he doesn't drop the mitts you are going to shove your thumbs through his nostrils and watch them come out his eye sockets. Sometimes the stupid hanging microphone picks up the comment, which then circulates on social media and you end up with a two-game suspension and a five-thousand-dollar fine. And how to explain that you are not actually a particularly violent person when what circulates on YouTube is a shot of you skating across the rink at full speed, holding two halves of a stick you've just broken over your knee, the ends like mouths full of jagged splintery fangs.

WHAT HAPPENED WITH STACEY, after the eyeball incident, was that I told her about Rebecca. After that fit of laughter I said I had to take off and she gave me that same look again, like wanting some wordless more, and I opened easy as a twist-off Chablis. Told her about Rebecca the gorgeous and brilliant and funny publicist for a women's health magazine. Her and me the high school sweethearts of Chemical Valley. Rebecca with the single snaggled incisor and a smile like a grade school secret. I told her about the diagnosis, a year after Lucy was born. Everything planned: five more years and going back home to Sarnia to run a hockey school or work for the Sting while Rebecca drove into the Toronto office two days a week. Told her about Rebecca's double mastectomy, how they found a colony of cysts on the uterus, meaning full hysterectomy plus radiation. How there was no sex for two years and then Rebecca went to the doctor concerned about something hanging out of her vagina and the doctor said it was her bowel. Seven hot nights hardly swallowing thinking over and over what kind of a man leaves the ovarian-cancer-surviving mother of his two-year-old child. Puking at practice and for the first time in my life unable to stomach food. I told Stacey all of it. Told her how Rebecca had calmly lowered her voice and said she'd always suspected I was a monomaniac and at least now she knew. Told her how Rebecca took the house and the child and half the bank account and though she'd always been against them she had new implants by the end of the week. How she called them a gift to herself. I told Stacey how that was three years ago now and my daughter was five and begging for a baby brother and I'd had this perfect chance to make a good family and had failed. I told every stained and sneering truth and she asked what my name was, my real name. Then she said we didn't have to do anything but could we just go to bed and she took me there, wrapped her fingers around my drugged, exhausted cock and just held it there, whispering, "Jay, Jay, Jay," until we both fell asleep.

THE PLANE LANDS in Boston at 4:00 which means straight to the bus because the puck drops at 7:30. On the ride to the rink Moose tells me coach is probably going to ask me to spar with Anderson, which both of us know is a bad idea. Not because me and Anderson were a regular d-pair for two seasons in Tucson—you fight your friends more often than not in this line of work. It's a bad idea because Anderson is soft. Because he got called up last month and he's won two fights and so his coach is foolish enough to think he can scrap. Because it's my first game back and there's no way, contract-wise, I can justify holding back but if I don't hold back somebody could get hurt. Somebody who's not me.

So I sit in the bus looking out across the river and thinking maybe that's Harvard on the other side. Moose tells me Anderson texted him saying I better get a broom because I'm going to get dusted which I'm not even sure makes sense. I try not to think about Anderson and eventually it works. I start thinking about Harvard, thinking maybe Lucy will go there one day, wondering what my daughter will think of me five years from now. Wondering if I want her to watch me tossing knuckles for a living. I'm thinking, not for the first time, that maybe retirement is my best option. Maybe I could try journalism or get a nice office job with the players' association. Maybe I could get into training, use my kin credentials. Maybe it would be nice to throw towels at guys and lay hurt players on spinal boards and stitch them up on the bench.

THERE ARE FEW THINGS as lovely as the sight of blood pooling on white ice. No red has ever seemed more red— like a rose blooming out of a snowbank. It is this sight, I sometimes think, that keeps me going. Not the ocean hush of the crowd, not the salary or the sense of belonging, not the elite-level gear or the hundred thousand Twitter followers but the sight of a man's liquefied essence spreading out before him. The gentle wisp of steam as it leaks onto the indifferent slab below. The pattern never the same and something so simple and vast about those spattered archipelagos on the cool, stark ice. Recalling, always, the same shrill memory. A childhood pond, a whirl of lazy snowflakes. Flakes like little white insects bobbing after each other and never quite getting there. Sweat-damp pant legs clinging to calves. The shred of skates *skirring* over ice. Cardinals fluttering through a winter sky.

WHAT HAPPENED WITH STACEY, eventually, is that she doesn't date hockey players. It's always been a rule of hers. An age-old prohibition she chose not to bring up until three weeks in. A steadfast embargo that did not prevent her from sitting in the special box reserved for wives and girlfriends and saying afterwards over rye and Cokes that she could get used to that kind of treatment. A hard-and-fast rule that did not deter her from joining me on one of my twice-monthly Sunday afternoons with my daughter. Did not discourage her from playing mini-put at the mall with me and Lucy, the three of us afterwards drinking Orange Julius in the food court, singing along in Kermit the Frog voices to the late-November Christmas music—"He sees you when you're sleeping / He knows when you're awake." This alleged rule didn't stop Stacey from coming back to my apartment and eating spaghetti while watching *Frozen*. From holding Lucy's hand under the blanket and then saying "I hope so" when Lucy asked whether she'd see her again. But it did cause her, a week later, to suddenly cease communication. To leave all texts and phone calls unanswered for three days and then finally write back, *I'm sorry, Jay, I can't date a hockey player. It's been fun but please don't contact me again.*

THERE ARE TIMES when there are no good choices. There are moments when you have to choose between your own happiness and your duties, your vows. What you may have to realize is that "sickness and health" can become very literal, very mundane. "Sickness and health" can mean you spend 90 percent of your waking life cleaning vomit and changing your baby's diapers and helping your impossibly pale wife stagger from the bathroom to the bed, her body like an apple tree in winter. It can mean walking over to a lump of covers and body holding that screaming infant several times a day and the child's mother always groaning back, "I can't I'm sorry I just can't," a morbid whistle wheezing through the back of her mouth where the chemo has rotted the teeth out. It can mean that since you have a decent salary you can afford a part-time in-home caregiver for when you have to practise and play and sometimes her mother comes down to help but none of this stops you from feeling terribly, constantly, excavated. Feeling like a grave that has been dug up and left open, exposed to the vagaries of sleet and snow and wind. A grave who has to rise up each morning to smile and bounce his never-silent child up and down the vicious beige halls.

And of course you know it's worse for Rebecca. Of course you do everything you can to imagine her side, to consider how she must feel when she can't feed or snuggle or even really touch her own child. You reach into every deepest reservoir of empathy but at some point it doesn't change the fact that something in you is faded, almost lost.

You may get through all of this because you simply couldn't gather the strength to leave in the middle of the sickness. You may come through everything to discover your beloved partner is weary and sexless and she is not making any promises because her underbits are all sliced up and swollen. You may find yourself mining for sympathy, desperate to be a good person but some nights you dream her saying "just go," saying "it's okay." And you can't anticipate that it will never be okay. You can't predict that leaving does not, in fact, mean relief.

How could you know that after leaving you would wake up each morning to find your tongue turning fuzzy and your stomach a mangle of rage and shame? How could you know you would look into your daughter's planetary eyes and wince with shame each time she said the word "mummy"? That the shame would thrill through your bloodstream and you would lie awake at night fearing the You your daughter will come to construct as she grows older. The You that has left his diseased and broken wife alone with their daughter and the ravage of her body. Fearing this future You because it is also present You and nothing, now, can make that otherwise.

ONE OF THE worst things is the waiting. Waiting through the plane ride and the bus from the airport and warm-up and the pre-game speech and the national anthem, knowing the whole time that you are going to have to get violent. Sitting on the bench listening to the crowd turning frenzied and knowing you've got to face a professional fighter who will open your face in an instant if you have a lonely second thought about pounding him first.

I sit on the bench feeling a little ridiculous wearing all this gear. I sit through the Megacard national anthem, sit through the Mite-T-Gel puck drop and the Trinity TV time outs, wondering when I'm going to get my nudge. Moose scores a clapper in the first and then they bang in three quick ugly ones and I'm sure I'm going to get the tap but I don't get the tap. At the start of the second we kill off a double minor and there's a long stretch of play with no whistles and then I see Anderson taking the ice. He's lining up on the wing and he's got his little weasel eyes on Taylor, which is when Coach grabs my shirt and basically hurls me over the boards.

At the faceoff circle, standard banter: "Let's get some Windex on that glass jaw." "Nice fuckin' lip sweater." "How're your glutes, bud? Picking up a few splinters from the pine wagon?"

Then Anderson goes personal, goes dark. "Shame about Rebecca," he says, nodding iceward. "Heard she got shredded down there, basically went through the blender."

Words that send the world listing.

A blast of light and a dentist's drill, sans anaesthetic.

Everything red and blue and all cares and friendships wilting and who the fuck did Anderson hear this from? My chest and biceps flickering and a slurge of vomit in my throat. A smell like oil and before I can swing the puck drops and Anderson skates away chuckling and I'm lost out here with the horn-blare and the crowd-howl and everything noisemakers, everything glare.

Bodies whizzing around and the *schwick* of skates on ice and I find myself with the puck even though the puck means nothing now. Thinking about shooting just to get rid of it but then I see Anderson and I simply leave the puck where it is, skate towards him dropping my stick and gloves.

WHAT HAPPENED WITH STACEY, eventually, is that I went to her house late-night. I drove over to her condo six and a half deep, fully ready to rage into her intercom and send some golf balls through her window. Expecting her to be in there with the latest Justin Tinderlake but no such luck or whatever else you'd call it. Because it turned out she was sweet, deadly sweet. Turned out she answered the intercom and said hey, said she'd half expected this, said she'd been thinking a lot about it and she supposed I deserved an explanation so come on up. So I came on up, mussed Gorgonzola until his eyeball made a move and then I sat there on the couch with my feet lost in zebra-print plush. She brought me a peppermint tea which I did not remotely drink and told me that although she'd told herself she wouldn't do it a friend had sent her a link which brought her down a YouTube rabbit hole. Hence she wound up watching me pommel guys. She spent a fierce half hour watching me flatten Denis O'Neil's nose and concuss Ryan Armstrong and blind Todd Salinger in one eye. And after seeing me batter people like that, she said, she could no longer look at me the same way. She just couldn't get those images out of her mind and that's why she hadn't responded to my texts—when my name came up she saw visions of me leering and ramming my arm down another man's throat, flashes of me skating down the ice holding two composite plastic scythes, my beard bright with blood. All of it made her squeamish and fearful, she said, and how could I possibly object? She saw me as a barbarian, i.e., saw me as myself and I could not argue with that so I walked out. Walked into the elevator and plummeted down. Fell slowly through the city with my feet on the floor.

ANDERSON TURNS and smiles for a second then sees that I'm bare-knuckled and drops his mitts. I'm swinging before they touch the ice. Two swings before he can even get his fists up and he's already down and tucking. I sit down hard on his chest and start beating, feel the teeth slough loose under my knuckles and keep going, opening his nose.

A hiss in my ears, someone far away whispering *mono-maniac*. A flash of a woman in silhouette, stark and bald at the bathroom sink.

My fists churn faster and as I look down Anderson's face becomes my face too. I'm torqueing my fists against my own face, watching my skull tock against the ice and my eyes go distant. I find myself split in two and know this can't be right but it does not make the warmth of the blood between my fingers less real. And even as I keep pounding I know that none of this is reversible, that this choice cannot be undone, and so there is nothing to do but keep swinging, keep trouncing, keep mashing this mask until it curdles, leaks the matter of its making.

DESERT
OF THE RL

DADDY ISSUES SAYS he wants to take her to the desert someday—Gobi, Jordan, Atacama. He thinks the desert is underloved, that more charismatic landscapes get all the hype but has she heard of salt flats, of pink flamingos, of the Valley of the Moon? Daddy Issues says our lives are whirlwinds of simulations, our morality built in consumer choices—Walmart sinners, thrift store martyrs, a redemption of organic kale. Daddy Issues doesn't use social media, refuses to milk data from his flesh. He wears plaid and vegan Blundstones, grooms his beard with fine-toothed sandal-wood. He has two long dimples above his pouting buttocks, likes to joke that his rear end is luscious with negative capabil-ity. Daddy Issues once described a maki roll as pedestrian. Most nights, he buzzes Carly into his one-bedroom above the McDonald's on Richmond Street, a lonely red IKEA bicycle on the wall among his paintings of pirate ships and giant squid and manga motorcycle starlets. As his floor fans turn their clicking heads, Daddy Issues talks about the street names in this transplant town—Adelaide, Oxford, Piccadilly, how the fuck do you pronounce Grosvenor? Waterloo, Wellington, Dundas, Tecumseh, the great chief, tokenized vestige of the world we've tarpapered into a parody England, pretending the displaced aren't still here. Daddy Issues is recently single after a five-year relationship with a woman who wanted him to get a so-called commitment vasectomy because she couldn't have children and how's that, he says, for a psychoanalyst's nocturnal emission? When she asks him why the apartment is so bare, Daddy Issues says it's because he wants to travel once he pays off his student loans and, incidentally, he recommends not leasing your mind to the STEM apologists. Daddy Issues left the academy to devote his life to art and yes tattooing is an art. Daddy Issues did half a masters at Western, ran out of funding writing a thesis on rogue AI and existential risk. When he told her this, Carly asked what he meant by funding and he told her about the acronyms, the councils, a colleague who'd gotten fifteen grand from OGS and spent it on a pony. She lay naked and sticky staring at his IKEA art picturing him in academic robes, riding over dunes, a degree in his mouth and needles in his hands.

CARLY DRIVES HOME past tan houses and clicking garage lights and teenage trees. She is not sure if she should call it dating, what she does with Daddy Issues. Six frothy weeks during which it has barely rained and they have not left the apartment. Carly is also not sure why she continues to think of him as Daddy Issues, a name which Aisha came up with when they were studying Freud in philosophy class because Ms. Katz is all gung-ho International Baccalaureate best standardized results in the province. Carly's father was nothing like Daddy Issues. He was a dentist from Singapore who'd lived a decade in San Antonio, moved north for dental school, believed that the true test of the permanent resident was to build your own canoe. But Aisha had called him Daddy Issues and asked was he handsome and she'd said handsome enough but it's not about that.

Pools glint moonlight as she wends the cul-de-sacs, sprinklers whirling over parched lawns. In front of every house squat boxes spin and spin, whisking crazed against the heat. Passing the park at the end of her street, the one that looks out over the man-made pond, she sees a goose in her rear-view. A goose in the middle of the road, possibly limping, glowing pink as she steps on the brake. She is always astonished by their size. As tall as a child, as her sister. Carly climbs out of the car, approaches the edge of the park, but the goose has crept into some shadow. She thinks to call to it but what could she say? So she watches a lone cloud breathe past, a slime of moon in the still pond.

She comes inside to find Gord chomping the head off a crown of broccoli. Sitting on the couch leg-spread and vein-necked in sweatpants while Grace watches *Peppa Pig*. Gord holds the broccoli by the stalk, eating straight from the head, a dandruff of green buds on his chest and thighs. He grunts hello as Carly scours the fridge, pulls out peanut sauce, rice, slides yesterday's pizza into the microwave. Peppa and her brother leap in mud puddles and Grace is boinging on the carpet, screaming, "Splish, Splash!" She's talking to no one about passing lorries and how she might have to wash her trousers.

The toilet flushes and their mother, Janet, appears with a new talk-to-the-manager haircut. "Where were you?"

"Aisha's."

"Sure," Janet says, pulling Chablis from the fridge. "Hot date?"

"Mum. Don't," Carly says, spinning away with her plate. Gord's hand is mining his sweatpants when she passes the couch. She slides him a look like gross and he grins, puts his palms up flat. "Just making sure they're still there."

Upstairs, in the thick heat of her bedroom, Carly eats her dinner and texts Aisha about Friday's zooms, the meme dance, potential costumes. The AC is broken again and her bedroom is a madness of sweat, a hot breeze trailing from the tiny window, a stinkbug buzzing on the sill in deranged circles. Carly and Aisha ping memes back and forth and then the conversation trickles and she is alone listening to bath time, Grace singing the songs from *The Lion King*, making "be prepared" into "Babybel."

She's staring at the photo above her door—her father's bald head gleaming over the barbecue, his thick chest clad in bikini-bod novelty apron—when Grace trots through the door in her hooded towel and starts climbing the bed. She slings a tiny leg up and stands shifting and struggling but when Carly moves to help her Grace shrugs her hand off.

Pleased with herself, Grace announces: "I want feel your heartbeep."

"Heartbeat." Carly smiles back. Grace nods factual, curls in beside her sister.

"Mum's making chocolate mousse."

Carly smiles, tells her here, crawls her sister's tiny fingers to the pulse on her neck. Her sister's brown eyes hover close, a smell of bath crayons and the sulphite smell of her *Frozen* shampoo. Grace curls into Carly's shoulder nook and Carly asks if she can feel it. Grace says yes like a question so Carly reaches up, digs two fingers in, feels with her sister the flow of blood below skin.

AISHA IS TALKING about her project on renewables as they walk through the parched suburbs on their way to the bus stop. They're walking through the sprinklers and bald lawns, glimpsing the jeweled blue of backyard pools and Aisha is talking about starlings, the millions of dollars of damage they do to farms each ear, how they're an introduced species, immune to the Migratory Bird Treaty Act. She's talking Blue Carbon and TuNur energy, a whole giant belt of solar panels across the deserts of Tunisia but all the energy goes to Europe. Carly says isn't she a barrel of laughs today and brings up the costumes but Aisha starts talking about the colonial history of grass. They're walking past the thirsty yellowed lawns and spinning sprinklers and Aisha says grass wasn't like this before colonization. She says there was sweetgrass, hair grass, switchgrass, but it was tall and wiry and it went to seed. They pass rain barrels and bumper sticker vegans and Aisha's saying about this weird carpet, pointing down at the lush green turf fat with chemical and purged of mycelium as they arrive at the stop. The bus pulls up and Carly is watching all the sun-streaked windshields blazing by, the shush of Richmond Street like a lost ocean and Aisha is saying about the roots reaching out, looking for something deeper, something to mix with, tangle into.

Aisha whirls her finger like selfie, so Carly scooches in, tilts her face. As the camera clicks, Carly wonders if the click sound is artificial. Lawns and cars whiz by, hungover students waddle in UWO sweatpants. She watches it all through her own pale reflection in the bus window. Aisha adjusts her teeth in Facetune, asks if they're too white.

Near the front of the bus Carly sees a man with a droopy stalactite of flesh hanging off his nose, a wobbly round growth as long as a thumb. She has seen him often on this route. Janet says he sits on the bus all day because he likes to have people look at it, the nose. Rides all day just hoping someone will stare at his nose as Carly does now, fixating on the swinging tear-drop pendulum as lawns blush by the windows. Carly is thinking about flamingos, about geese in artificial ponds. Thinking past the sound walls and into the lawns of the suburbs, chlorine pumping into pools.

Aisha closes Facetune, tries CreamCam. Carly sits watching her friend's flesh change shades, her blemishes fade. In the back of the photo sits the man with the growth on his nose, trapped in the space between their two grinning faces. "God." Aisha huffs. "I hate my skin."

AT HOME THAT NIGHT, Carly looks up the TuNur solar project. Fleets and fleets of panels sprawling over the desert, a thousand square mirrors gleaming, cloaked in heat-shimmer. She saves the picture and makes it her background, her home screen, lies staring at the sun-gorged desert on the far side of the icons as night falls. She wonders what it looks like from space, if an astronaut could see this sequined belt on the waist of the world.

CARLY MET DADDY Issues at the Starbucks counter, waiting for her mocha. "Charlie," the barista said, and they both reached for the same cup. He had a GoodLife bag slung over his shoulder, his arms jungled with tattoos. Swirls of green, red, and black that reminded her of a book she read to Grace about a boy named Max with a jungle in his room. He looked at her hard, cracked into a smile. There were three grey hairs in his beard, a few lines around his eyes. He could have been twenty, or thirty.

"Nice to meet you, Charlie."

"That's just my Starbucks name. It's easier."

"Good choice." He grinned. He told her his real name was Gilles but people couldn't say it right. "They say it like gills, likes a fish's gill." His tongue searched out of his mouth, flashed its silver eye. When he asked, she told him her real name.

"I like your tattoo," she said, pointing to one at random, surprising herself.

"Want one?"

She shrugged, meaning yes.

"Come with me."

They walked the dirty sidewalks, ignored the people asking for change. Outside the shop he pulled out a thick ring of keys. Adult keys. She was humming with fear and want. He turned the lights onto gnawed leather chairs, fat binders on the counter, home-drawn manga on the crimson walls. He took her upstairs, through a black lace curtain, patted the bench. "Don't worry," he said, pulling the plastic off the needles. "It's all safe." He grinned. "What do you want?"

"Maybe a raven?"

He laughed and she saw that his teeth were tenderly stained. "A dandelion with the fluff floating away?"

"Maybe some Cantonese characters?"

"But you can't know what they mean." He chuckled, turned the needle on. "Okay," he said. "I know. Where do you want it?" She rolled over, pulled her shirt up. "You'll have to take it off."

As he worked, he told her about the parts that hurt more, about shading and linework and colour, about the ditch and the different thickness of needles he could use. She lay prone on her stomach, his knee pushed into the cushion, his thigh against her hip. She stared at the photos of tattooed Minotaurs and pirate ships and full-back dragons on the walls, but found herself drawn to the needles in the garbage can—a thick black garbage bag and all those needles piled in a tangled mess and she wondered where they would all end up, imagined them on the sea floor, a kind of coral of glass and steel. Aisha had showed her photos of these artificial reefs in the states, abandoned New York City subway cars dropped into the ocean and blooming into a kind of aquatic drag show—covered in seaweed and algae, mussels hitching to them, octopuses building troves inside. In the photos they looked like little vegetal houses, their green hats swaying in the current.

"You sat well," he said when he was finished. He brought a hand-held mirror over, stood her in front of the other one, shirtless in the stark light. Two finger smudges haunted the mirror's fringe. He asked what she thought and she stared into the mirror, told him it was beautiful, which was true. She didn't tell him the other part: that she was glad it would live in a place no one could see.

IN THE MORNING she goes to the kitchen window and watches Gord weed the lawn, pluck the heads off dandelions. Around the neighbourhood lawn mowers roar, sprinklers gleek. As a child she thought dandelions had something to do with *The Wizard of Oz*, begged to meet the dandy lion. Gord often brags about his Par 4, the special fertilizer he gets from his friend who manages a golf course. "Technically illegal," he grins at strangers nodding from the curb. Most years, their lawn is dizzy with green. Now Gord stoops over the ragged yellow scree, pulls weeds up with his head stooped. Holds the yellow heads in his hands and stoops to stare at them, as if they were a reckoning.

Spinning away from the window, Carly grabs her phone wrong, watches it tumble slow-mo. She reaches through dreamy moment, swipes the phone but instead of clasping it she jams it straight into the corner of the counter. She knows before looking, confirms a white seam down the middle. A ragged tear through the deserts of Tunisia, a frayed belt of busted glass.

IN PHILOSOPHY CLASS, Holly leans over whispering about the zooms, the plans to trip pre meme dance. Mrs. Katz asks if she'd like to share with the class and she says she's supposed to meet some real fun guys on Friday. Giggles and snorts peal through the classroom. Mrs. Katz stands with her hands on her hips, her body saying not funny, a sliver of mirth in her eye.

Mrs. Katz does her assignment-time desk tap and everyone starts pulling out their Chromebooks. Mrs. Katz asks the students write out our social media philosophy, so I open a Word doc and sit staring out into the green sweep of June, thinking about Daddy Issues, what he said about meme-stitched selves. She sits thinking about how kids get a bad rep for their phones, her English teacher called them the "head-down tribe" but the adults she knows are the worst offenders—Gord, her mother, her grandfather. She looks over at Aisha's page: "The Dick Pic Era." Holly's screen just says "Pics or It Didn't Happen." IB philosophy, the pride of Central Collegiate. Keys clack like plastic rain.

Outside her locker, Holly flashes the baggie, the little brown mottle like an embryo. Black brain, white limbs. The plan is Holly's house—she has a private basement with her own door. They discussed MDMA, but decided organic was safer. None of them has tried shrooms before.

"How bad could it be?"

"It's only poison." Holly grins.

GRACE IS GREENPEACING, their mother's term for a toddler lying on her back and screaming inconsolably. Grace wailing in this case due to a failed chocolate mousse experiment. Weeks of chocolate mousse this, chocolate mousse that, and now tears and abjection because the expectation was moose. Because where is the moose, Grace pleaded, tear-swollen, pointing at her favourite antlered plush toy and then descending into speechless rage, sobbing and howling, her face smeared with leakage, snot and spit mingling, the child barely able to manage a breath until Carly appears, kneels beside her sister.

"It's all right," she tells her sister, herself. "Should we take a bath?"

"Okay." Grace sniffs, rising up, taking her sister's hand and following her to the tub.

They pour *Frozen*-brand bubbles into their pseudo-porcelain vessel. Carly produces Scuba Steve and the pink plastic narwhal/unicorn, the plastic yogurt tubs and the bath colours and the bath crayons. They watch the water pour. Carly grabs some toilet paper, blows her sister's nose. Grace grabs the footstool and proudly pees, farts, grins, her cheeks still red. They climb in and contemplate the square faucet noses, the plugged drains. Carly tells her sister about the secret city inside, where benevolent house sprites live. Grace puts her head in Carly's lap, leans back and kicks, brags that she's swimming. Her scalp warm, her brown hair dark and flowing like tendrils. Grace crawls behind her, starts splashing with joy. "Tattoo!" she cries, astonished. For her birthday, Carly received a crate of stick-on Peppa Pigs, covered an entire leg with cartoon pink.

"Don't tell Mum."

Grace giggles, runs her fingers down the river of her sister's spine. Rubs harder and harder, as if she could scrub it off. "It's so big," she says. "Bigger than my hand!"

Carly spins into her sister's joy.

"Will I be as big as you someday?"

"Yes," she says.

Grace swims around to the front, thinking hard about this. She sits in the bath, slumped and wide-eyed and pondering. "When I'm as big as you, will you be as little as me?"

Carly wants to laugh but doesn't. Instead, she just shrugs, says maybe, cuddles her sister and runs her fingers through her hair. Their mother appears, thanks in her eyes, wine in her hand, and Carly imagines herself shrinking. She thinks her sister growing, sprouting, while she shrinks smaller and smaller, as little as her sister and then even more tiny until she is insectile, until she can swim into the faucet, seek the secret cities in the deep unseen.

HER FATHER USED to take her walking along the river trail. They'd stand on bridges and stare down and watch the water, full and fierce in spring, tired and brown in August. The shore strewn with tossed vacuums and televisions, the sparse woods on the river's fringe thick with tents and stomped needles. It smelled like grass and earth and the green goose turds nested in the grass, like the distant roar of Mustangs. Sometimes they saw beavers near the bridge or possums dipping in and out or a turtle sunning on a rock beside a tire. Always there were ducks that would waggle over but her father said they shouldn't feed them. One spring day they went down and the goslings were out, golden creatures waddling after their mothers in perfect lines and how astonishing it was that they could start so lovely and end so mean and grey. They'd walked down toward the river forks and he had bought her a Popsicle and they sat on a bench in a blizzard of little yellow-white tufts, tufts that she was sure were bits of gosling feather but he said no, it was from the plants. He must have seen her wither because he reached around and squeezed her, held his palms out to catch the off-white snow and said what did it matter where it came from it was certainly magic. She didn't know if he was right but what mattered was the trying and so she tilted into the lean of him, set her ear into his chest and heard his heart beating somewhere in the beneath of him as she watched the pollen flit and flirt and the water cannon spat up and up, the water climbing and arcing and finally tumbling into the river far below.

DADDY ISSUES is telling her about the desert of the real as she stares up at the red IKEA bicycle in sepia Paris, the fans clicking all around her. The AC is on but it doesn't work right, can't fight the heat, and Daddy Issues is saying about the French philosopher who inspired that line from *The Matrix* and it's weird, right, because what it means is that the real is impoverished but Daddy Issues doesn't think that's fair to deserts. The symbolism is barren, parched, inert but what he thinks about is tar bush and prickly pears and agave, lizards and cats crawling the dunes at night. He thinks about groundwater, about the streams running beneath the sand because life is always there you just have to look for it.

She shows Daddy Issues her broken phone and he pinches it like dirty underwear, asks why we even call these things phones. She shrugs and stares at the ceiling where the traffic lights smear green, change to red as Daddy Issues starts talking about "pics or it didn't happen," what that really means. He asks don't people see the irony of something not being real until there's a simulation of it? She ponders this, looking up at the bicycle, then at the McDonald's light playing in the small wall mirror next to the front door. She knows he will answer his own question, and he does so quickly. Tells her it's because technology moves faster than language. She stares into his neck tattoo, Marvin the Martian tilting his blaster, wondering if language isn't a technology too. Around her the fans whiz and turn, huge as black steel sunflowers.

Daddy Issues asks what she wants to do tonight and she says ice cream, meaning outside, public. He thinks hard, too hard, and she wants to remind him that they're consenting adults since she turned eighteen.

They go to Dairy Queen, where she orders them an Oreo Blizzard with two spoons. She sees him looking around, eyes switching. When the counter boy turns the ice cream upside-down he flinches, arm shooting out to grab it.

"It's all right." She laughs. "You've never had a Blizzard?"

"That's not ice cream," he says.

"Come on. You can't be that old."

"I didn't say I'd never had one. I said that's not ice cream."

"No." She gleams. "It's delicious."

THURSDAY IS DAD'S birthday, meaning Carly stays home from school and watches *P.S. I Love You* with Janet, the two of them weeping into delivery macchiatos. Grace is at daycare and Janet is "working" from home, moving the mouse around on her laptop every so often and doing two half-hour video calls in pyjama bottoms and a cowl neck. After the movie Janet tosses the quilt off, the tongues of her ancient Garfield slippers wagging, and asks if Carly is okay these days. Carly nods, puts a hand on her mother's knee, and says don't worry she's not pregnant.

They shower and eat and then they drive north through the tan suburbs, the yellow excavators and huge mounds of dirt of the future suburbs. They pass the dam and get to the bend in the river where, five years ago, they opened the urn. Carly thinks of how heavy it was, the surprising heft of ash. She remembers hearing the word "earn" every time someone said "urn." Aisha was there, squinting out over the water, crying although she barely knew him. They'd been in the same grade all their lives but that year they'd gotten close, bonded over scrunchies and metal straws. Carly was at Aisha's house for a sleepover the day she got the call—Janet's shuddery voice on the other end. When Janet picked Carly up, Aisha slid into the car beside her friend, held her hand and wept openly, fearlessly, in a way Carly still hasn't managed.

Today there's a firepit and some broken beer bottles and a crazed goose screaming around a fallen tree up the river. Carly sits down and lets the cold wind whip hair over her eyes. She lets the tears come into her vision, watches the way the world changes, wobbles, flexes. She breathes, like the counselor said, into the pain. Then she notices the trees. They're different, bigger. Gnarled pines where she remembers alder and young oak. The goose snorts, blares, honks and honks until the sound seems to bend into the word "wrong." The bird takes off flying, snorting through the sky, comes back again, lands on the river in a hectic flutter. "Must have lost her young," Janet says, picking up brown shards of glass and setting them in a paper bag.

The evening is virgin margaritas and sneaking tequila in and Gord slinking her mother off to bed. Carly moves the icons aside on her laptop, staring into the cracked desert of her home screen. She messages Aisha and Daddy Issues but neither of them answer so she lies on the couch thumbing through her father's Facebook photos: At the office in his white coat, holding his scaler and dental mirror, staring solemn into Janet's mouth. Holding up a giant foam finger at Carly's first hockey game, the one where she lay down across the goal mouth and recorded a shutout. She scrolls back and back through time—a Viking dinner, Christmas in San Antonio before her grandmother died. A visit to Singapore where she and her father climbed a hill into a park and he started crying watching a group of men practicing Silat. Soft quiet tears and he took his glasses off and folded them, slipped them into the pocket of his math-teacher plaid shirt. The hotels on the waterfront in their sleek insectile glory and she wanted to ask why was he crying but never got the nerve.

DADDY ISSUES GREETS her shirtless and grinning, teeth glowing and spotty from a recent bleach kit experiment. He's wearing only underwear and pulls her right into the bed but she's relieved that he doesn't have expectations today, that the underwear must be for the heat. She doesn't ask about his new tan, just leans into his chest, listens to a thud in the depths, two tall floor fans pivoting their heads, necks clicking. He puts on some tortured indie and he says he's sorry he forgot—work has been busy, there's some drama with his ex. He says he can talk if she wants him to fill the air, or he can listen. She shrugs, says quiet is best and so he holds her and she coils into him, strokes his beard and stares at the red bicycle and the giant squid and the leather-suited woman on her motorcycle. She gets a Coke from his fridge and drinks it slow, thinking of distant sugar canes.

Usually they don't talk about her high school social life but tonight, face gooey in the McDonald's light, he asks her if she's going to the meme dance tomorrow. She says yes and he asks what her costume will be, so she tells him about it, surprised he's never heard of the uncanny valley. She tells him about her online foray into Freud and the uncanny and robotics, how the android seems likeable until it gets too human, crosses the valley. And she tells him that for some reason she always imagined it as a real valley sort of like *Tron*—blue and red lights, a vintage future.

He grins, chuckles into the ceiling. "Sounds like your next tattoo."

A thought congeals: "But don't we all sort of live there?"

"Where?"

"Uncanny valley?"

He strokes her forehead, tells her she's not like other girls her age. She stares back at him stunned, curious, waiting for him to notice. He goes to the bathroom, moves the fans around, comes back and plays *Tron* on his laptop and they smoke a slim joint and she wakes up at 2:00 a.m., tongue mummified, the IKEA bicycle spinning lurid on the wall. Her mother has texted. The dark is too thick, too close. Daddy Issues's body heat glows sour beside her. The bicycle on the wall is a fierce, vivid red. The traffic lights on the ceiling turn from red to green and someone shouts from the street corner: "The end is nigh—get high!"

He stirs as she puts her jeans on. "Where are you going?"

"Home."

"I'll walk you."

"I'm driving."

He rolls over.

She drives home wondering how this was supposed to make her feel. She thinks of geese, of Grace, of flamingos, of malls. She would have liked to ask him: what are they like, girls her age? She would have liked to be meaner, tougher. Garage lights click in the cul-de-sacs as she passes the man-made lake. Sees, she is sure, something wobble in the shadow of a tree.

She finds her mother sitting at the kitchen island, dead sober. "Where've you been?"

"Aisha's."

Her mother holds her phone up, but Carly doesn't need to read the green bubbles or the blue ones. Seeing Aisha's father's name is enough. "Who is he?"

"No one."

Her mother shifts.

"Tell you later."

"No shit."

HOLLY IS DRESSED in cat ears, whiskers drawn on her cheeks, and she's passing the grog and heating hot knives on the stove and asking if anyone's feeling it yet. She has NONONO written on her forehead, though the makeup is already starting to leak in the heat. A novelty tail trails out of her jeans and she walks around swinging it and rolling her eyes, staring into the tea in her hand. She sips and grabs a spoon, pulls up some of the shroom grog in the bottom and says she's thirsty, real parched. She does wild eyes and makes her voice gravelly and says she feels like the bog monster, thirsting for grog.

She slurps and passes to Aisha, impeccable as Old School Dwayne—jeans, fanny pack, gold chain, counter lean. Aisha sips and nibbles and passes to Carly, who stares into the wet sogg at the bottom of the travel mug as Holly tells her this part is essential, the grog is by far the most potent, time to ingest. The tea was one thing, but this is a new species of dank. A dank that slimes her tongue, slurps rotten into her guts, a taste like sawdust on her lips. It's only poison, she thinks as Aisha takes out a bottle of SoCo and cranks Peggy Gou and announces two truths and a lie which means, inevitably, Carly lying about Daddy Issues, telling the truth about Daddy Issues, telling the truth about Gord eating full crowns of raw broccoli. Lana is singing about Norman Rockwell and Aisha passes Carly the blades and she spills a hot rock onto her jeans, sits there watching it burn, not knowing what to do until Holly grabs it with her bare fingers, flings it hissing in a glass of ice water. Carly tells the truth about the bleach kit, about his ex. She lies about the pony, tells the truth about the girls-your-age comment at which point Aisha goes nasty. "He fucking said that?"

"What does he look like anyway?"

Aisha grins: "Let's creep him."

"He doesn't have social media," Carly says, and it's only when she says it aloud that it becomes suspicious and possibly absurd. It's only when Holly grabs her phone and searches *tattoo artists London Ontario* and asks is that him that it makes sense that he would have a second house, a house with cottage porn and family photos on the walls and of course that is him in a tracksuit at the playground, of course that's his beard with three grey hairs like a mutilated spider. Standing with his stately wife with twins in the stroller, the wife with droopy graceful eyes eating red and green Goldfish, the whole family biting from the same monstrous double banana split.

"Shit," a voice says.

"Are you all right," says another, and she is, of course she is, because it was only ever a delusion. She is all right but she is also on the bottom of a strange ocean, an ocean where the weeds are stringy and sick, lurid shades of blue.

"It's fine," she insists. "I'm fine," she says, rising, staggering stumbling, shivering and it is not so much the betrayal as the shift in the terms, in the ground. The walls are blue, she notices. A trembly, teardrop blue and Holly is saying tracers, saying shit, saying peak. Holly is laughing and Aisha is saying no this is serious and Carly is saying she'll be fine. Holly looks at her phone and begins to laugh wretchedly, asking Aisha to read the message and is her mother coming home. Aisha gigglingly confirms and so the girls are grabbing blue bags and packing up bottles and Carly's stomach is turning, trawling and it's only poison, only poison as they flee the basement and walk out into the hot wash of Talbot, the sky ravenous for rain and a thin breeze coming up from the river, shouts from downtown and she is okay, she tells Aisha and yes she is sure but look at those lights. The traffic lights. They are out of control and can you hear those pigeons and I just saw someone riding a bicycle with no head he had no head I swear.

She drops her phone and picks it up, stares into the broken desert. She scrolls through the contacts, considers his name, looks at the photos but can't look because she's nauseated as they arrive at the thumping school. Aisha and Holly find friends and Carly stands at the fringes among the smokers in a soup of loss and want not knowing where the drugs end. She stands next to a Kermit with teacup in the suffering dank of a desire that makes fools of us all as Ryan Brady jangles her cans and says, "Hey there uncanny girl," and she tries to smile like *Ha ha but don't get too close*. In the gym window she sees the slinging disco ball and she knows she can't go in, can't possibly enter that donjon of smoke-machine smell and strobing pulse and snuck mickeys and melancholy boners and so she is walking into the grass. Walking alone into the dark lush of the soccer field, so prim and tame and Aisha shouting is she okay and of course she is. Of course she is fine because she's kicking her shoes off and isn't it dank bliss the feel of the soil on her back, her fingers in the grass like a creature. The girls shouting after her and she says she'll come inside in a minute so they giggle off and she lies there feeling the turf like a hairy creature, rubbing each trimmed blade and she is sorry, she whispers and her knuckles stumble on some tufts. Soft balls that she grabs and finds to be the half-decayed heads of dandelions and she is sinking into a cool violet fear when her phone beeps and of course it's him, asking if she wants to come over after the dance. It's Daddy

Issues texting casually and the reading makes her sicker, sweatier, but he's saying he hopes she's safe.

She doesn't write back. She simply rises, walks through the turf careless of her shoes because the earth is cool on her feet and then she's jangling over the sidewalk, tinkling uncanny across Richmond, past the cyclists and the pawn-shop prowlers, a man pawing the sidewalk for cigarette butts. She walks past the closed thrift stores and used book-stores, glancing at her reflection in the windows—barefoot and lank-haired, cans stitched to her black T-shirt. She turns up Talbot, walks past hooting frat boys, past a legion of knee-high green bins that shudder gently and she can see inside to where the worms and flies work the compost. She watches a raccoon cross the road, stop to gaze at an oncoming car, its eyes yellow cauldrons.

At home, thankful that the lights are off, she sits on the back steps thinking of her mother, of Gord, of the alien hotels on the Singapore waterfront. There are solar-pow-ered supertrees there now, luminous vertical gardens, an airport with a forest inside. She opens her palm and finds the dandelion there, crushed and sweaty and ragged. She rubs its flesh into her palms, grabs her phone and stares at the gut-rot string of his messages. Is she all right? Where is she? Does she want him to pick her up? The messages turn-ing worried or jealous and she braves the screen's nausea long enough to delete the messages and block his number before creeping inside, taking the faucet by its stainless-steel neck and swiveling it for a kiss. The kitchen alive with ticks and hums. The *Tron*-bright blue of the digital clock. In the bathroom, she turns on a light. Looks at herself for a long time in the mirror. She turns the bath on, lets it run as she watches the streetlamps glowing orange on the window, stares into the small wall mirror where a woman stands. Lank hair, a blade of grass slumped on her brow, soil smudged up her neck. She thinks of Gilles, of the goose, of deserts and oceans, giant synthetic trees glimmering over the ocean and she sees that the real is an oozing thing, fluid and layered. She thinks of the grog, of the fungi rotting inside her, pulping in her stomach juices, seeping into her blood. She closes her eyes and sees dunes jeweled with solar panels, a bright red bicycle flying through the night and she knows that if the real is a desert there are rivers in its guts.

She tenses, hearing footsteps, floorboards, the door swinging open slow. She thinks her mother, or, worse, Gord. She looks for her mother's face and then down to the pink pyjamas, the soft brown curls, the tiny rolls of fat around the wrists. Her sister stands there squinting. "What's wrong?"

"Nothing."

"You dirty."

Carly laughs as her sister approaches, tests the water, stands contemplating it for a long time. Carly squirts water between her hands and her sister giggles, peels off her pyjamas, heaves a leg up with great difficulty and wiggles proudly into the bath. Grace leans her back into Carly's bare chest, asks Carly to tell her a story.

Once upon a time there was a mean man, a man with a lot of tattoos and three grey hairs in his beard and this man had two lives, two houses. "Two houses?" Grace gasps, turning around, eyes bright. "Two families? He must be really big."

Carly chuckles, squeezes her sister, takes a handful of bathwater and lets it run between her fingers as the first light creeps pink on the window. Her sister thumbs a clump of dirt from Carly's brow, says "wow" again and Carly reclines into the sound, the water, the poison and the joy and the grope of word for world.

SHTF

"WHEN THE POWER goes out," Geoff says, hefting the hay-bale-sized Amazon box from the doorstep, "you're going to be one lucky fellow." He waddles through the hallway, struggling with the heavy box, Zambonis our junk mail off the kitchen island. I help him peel the box open, glance in and see the label: *Firman Start Gas Portable Generator*.

"Did you buy that to show off to the Chili Preppers?"

"No, Zane." He tears the box open, links of clear plastic pillows. "I bought it to protect you." He turns from the generator long enough to peck me, his deep brown eyes prep-giddy. I stare at the word "Amazon," thinking of rainforests, decide against asking him where he's going to get his gasoline once the power goes out.

We eat ravioli with pesto cream sauce, drink gin and tonics. Geoff only has eyes for his generator. "Jenny," he says into his cocktail.

"What?"

He stands, lovingly strokes the generator. "We'll call her Jenny."

"You're cute."

The doorbell rings and I rise, swallow, dispense polite hellos, pulp guacamole as the Red Hot Chili Preppers slink in. Their real name is the Survive Tribe; the Chili Preppers is a running joke left over from when Geoff's prepping started, just after he lost his licence, when I still thought the habit was a quirk.

Pete shows up first, followed by Larry, toting a stuffed bugout bag. Pete's a surplused gym teacher; Larry's a retired cop. As I mash avocado, the preppers discuss extreme cold sessions, solar generators, silky saws, survivorcords.

Unlike Geoff, I am weary with ruins. Four decades ago my parents left their dammed city on the Nile where my mother spent her evenings hand-painting the eye of the resin scarab, the wings of coroplastic Isis. My quarrier father used to joke that he'd almost named me "baksheesh." We lived, poorly, off the relics of pharaohs millennia dead.

Tonight, Larry's presenting on survivalist food innovations. "Indigenous plant knowledge, sure, crucial," he says, brandishing a Mason jar of what appears to be rice. "But what are you going to do when that shit starts to rot?"

Setting the guacamole on the table with a bowl of blue tortilla chips, I see that the rice in Larry's jar is squirming, wriggling, is not rice.

"Larvae." He glows, holding the jar aloft. "Premium black soldier fly. I'm building a farm in the yard." He wags the jar around the room. "Insect protein is the future. Any guinea pigs?"

Geoff shakes his head. Pete stares into the faux-Persian IKEA rug. Larry grins wider, turns to me: "Zane?"

"Sure." I shrug, sitting down at the table. "How bad can it be?"

Geoff straightens in his seat, a splotch of guac on his upper lip. Larry hands me the Mason jar and I swirl it, staring into the larvae as they climb, crawl, trade places. Swarming, churning. I wonder what they're thinking, feeling, as they wriggle in the reedy yellow bodies of their kin. Skin to skin, flesh to flesh. Naked, thoughtless, immersed.

I open the lid and plop three or four in my mouth, work through two or three showy chews. The taste is like dirt, like earth. It's been a long time but the memory flashes through me of eating ants with my sister, thumbing them off the hot sidewalk. The taste barely detectable, faintly saline.

Geoff looks at me, thrilled. "What does it taste like?"

"Nutty? Could use some garlic butter."

The preppers cackle. Geoff grabs the jar and stares into the larvae. The talk turns to iodine tablets, syringes, tweezers, tubs of Vaseline. I excuse myself, claiming work.

What Geoff can't know is that I ate the larvae because I'm doing some prepping of my own. Because the last six months have been a series of tests—books laid out on coffee tables, invitations to mindfulness sessions, forwarded job openings, college programs in carpentry, in landscape design, urban planning, the Sommelier Certification Program. Geoff can't know that I am leaving. Perhaps tonight, perhaps tomorrow. That I have already bought a Trek 520, complete with paniers and a lightweight tent. He can't know that I have a new phone—new number, copious data, sufficient to connect my laptop as needed. He's already lost too much—his practice, his dignity, his century home with quartz countertops. I'll miss my gym, my geraniums, my horsehair exfoliation brush, my sandalwood shaving cream, the way Geoff slurps the crema from his espresso.

Passing through the kitchen, I eat a piece of dark chocolate, gaze through the window into the garden, where a squirrel perches on the fence above the composter, shivering as it gnaws the gnats off its tail. A statistician by trade, wildfires provide my sustenance. I model propagation axes and reaction pathways, use anisotropic smoothing to map rates of spread. As data, fire is a unique fascination—non-linear, irreversible, dizzyingly variable. The data on Geoff is more predictable. A gradual increase in time and money spent prepping, a significant decline in attention to the everyday workings of the world.

IT STARTED WITH CLOROX. Sodium hypochlorite, Geoff would stress. And he would be right. It is the same chemical, but Clorox doesn't own it. In dental surgeries like root canals, aqueous sodium hypochlorite solution ($NaOCl$) is a commonly administered rinsing solution, effective against microbiota. The problem is not rinsing with sodium hypochlorite; the problem is when you confuse your needles, mixing solution and anaesthetic. The problem is a fifty-three-year-old woman with sudden acute pain, severe swelling, blockage of airways, the assistant screaming, the dentist injecting more of what he thinks is anaesthetic, which is in fact $NaOCl$, leading to hospitalization and minor stroke, leading to lawsuits, to copious damages, to bankruptcy, a feral media response, and the complete possible bureaucratic ire of the National Dental Examining Board of Canada.

Shortly after the settlement, Geoff took a trip to Costco, came home with extra-large bags of rice. Lentils, batteries. I searched his browser history: Omniprep, Born Ready, Dare 2 Prepare. "Just in case," he said. "You never know." He began talking about SHTF events, and I had to search the definition. I thought it was temporary, a play for control, a way to staunch the rush of ruin. He had never been wild for dentistry, but he had been good at it. Now his career was gone, his sustenance and retirement and faith in himself compromised in a single misread vial. The foundations of his life exposed as fragile, porous, fleeting. Fearful and wounded, he nursed his hurt with cable ties, tinder, duct tape, lamp oil, paracords.

What is the line between madness and obsession?

It escalated fast: our house bulging with bugout bags, crates of matches, hydration tablets, high-grade LED flashlights, Mylar bags, five-gallon buckets with gamma-seal lids, sugar, honey, beans, oats. I made him promise not to buy any guns or ammunition. He said no, no, of course not, but what about a pellet gun? We agreed on flares. One day he took me out for a training run, carrying twelve bricks in his backpack. "Prepping is useless if you don't practice," he'd said. He began to spend more and more time on the Survive Tribe's YouTube channel, all of them watching each other's videos, commenting, praising, pushing. He started repeating rehearsed lines, explaining that a good prep knows to be always ready, to never double-dip the gear. When I asked, one morning, what exactly he was prepping for, he started talking about the Pareto 80/20 rule for emergency preparedness, the law of the vital few.

Once, a few months in, I told him I was getting concerned. He assured me it wasn't like that, it wasn't crazy. "I'm a common-sense prepper," he said, his eyes fixed on his screen. "It's not crazy; it's totally rational." On his iPad: a blog called *Prepared Housewives*. I turned his tablet face down. "I'm serious. I'm worried," I told him.

"You should be," he said, and his eyes went sharp as he waved a hand towards the outside world, the disaster that could strike at any time. Was already striking.

I HEAR THE preppers recording YouTube videos, and then their glum goodbyes. I wait for Geoff to come into the bedroom but instead I hear him leave the house. I rise, drift into the living room. Lie on the couch holding my iPad, tapping at a game of chess.

Staring at the checkered blur after losing a lazy endgame, I remember the larvae, pulped, now, in a surf of gut flora. I think of the jar, the brood, the larger industrial larvae farm they must have come from, and find myself recalling the cockroaches of my youth. My memories of Aswan are a blur of fūl and plastic sphinxes, of sailboats tacking in the reservoir, of baskets flush with duqqa, of Nubian tile, papyrus, sugar cane, stooping palms and the desert beyond. But in the midst of that fragrant dream: cockroaches. Rust-red cockroaches raining from the roof of the market. A cloud of them falling from the sky, landing on the sun-beat pavement, a blur of wing and antenna, of spiny legs and twitching wings.

A breeze from the river and the smell of garbage from the curb and the roaches in their hundreds tumbling, scuttling, clacking, a mound of writhing bodies clambering over and against one another, plummeting from the top of the pile, landing prostrate on the sidewalk, wings flexing, forelegs scuttling useless, seeking purchase on the air.

Geoff opens the door and peeks in. In his hands, a bright red jerry can. "Test drive?"

"Not in the living room."

"'Course not." He begins to drag the generator towards the back door. I ask when he's coming to bed and he tells me soon. For a moment, I long to tell him, to reach out, to detail the inventory of my hurt. Instead, I leave him to his preparations, his calculus of doom. I sip my tea, head back to the bedroom. Outside, the generator sputters and roars.

I MET GEOFF at a brew pub, drinking, our tongues furry with hops. We sat side by side at a long table with friends from the neighbourhood. Our shoulders brushed together, and he smiled. I complimented his teeth. "Crowns," he said.

"How imperial."

He laughed—gleaming, strapping, ursine. I asked him why there were so many dentists in London, a jawsmith on every corner. "It's the water." He winked. "We pay the city to put simple syrup in it."

In the bathroom, I watched him wash his hands, one finger at a time, with meticulous grace. Outside I found him leaning over a kind of novelty carnival fence, watching the great steel brewery vats, the air heady with malt. "I've been waiting for you," he confessed.

The next morning, he woke me with lavender chai, took me through his garden, squatted and ran his fingers through a lock of rosemary. "Smell this," he said, and I let his hands brush against my nose. In the quiet of his percale sheets, I ran my fingers over the ruined beds of his thumbnails, thought of those fissures as a kind of private Braille. At our boutique farmhouse wedding my parents sat with his, the four of them giggling, giddy, making plans to play bridge. The bartenders served Campari sodas, the barn flashing with highball sunsets.

Within a year we'd bought a house with a church-key window, our garden greedy with bougainvillea. "Curb appeal," our jovial realtor said, sweeping a palm across the flagstoned lawn. Gently, I put my thumb in Geoff's belt loop. Geoff was a dentist, but he wanted to retire early, to sell his practice. He talked of a vineyard, was already down to three days a week.

It wasn't just the way he swirled his Zinfandel, the honeymoon in Turkey—scrubbed together in hammams, ascending in hot-air balloons at sunrise, staring out over the dunes, the gorges, the olive trees. It was the quality, the depth, of his attention. I had been with many men, a few women. I'd been married once before. Yet I'd never felt a regard so sure—his steady eyes on my lips as I spoke about fire whirls and hydrology, his hand on my lower back as I knotted my tie. He was there, fiercely there, as if he'd opened every pore in me and come spilling reckless through.

GEOFF CURLS INTO bed beside me, the great heat of him. My furnace. He leans in, bends his head into my shoulder crook, musses the gruff of his stubble on my chest. I watch the slow churn of the ceiling fan, his eyelids flickering against my chest, his snore thickening, finding its stride.

I read, once, that despite popular claims, cockroaches would not survive heavy doses of radiation. The cockroach, in fact, is a hugely variable animal. There are 4,800 known species, only a handful of them pests. I read about their complex social structure, their sonic array, their kin recognition, meta-population structure, mating rituals, and dependence on common shelter. Yet, while the scarab was praised, the cockroach has been universally loathed and detested—a pestilence, a plague, killed en masse. How committed, we are, to branding pestilence. What a pretty fiction, these mandibled talismans of doom.

We wake abruptly in the shaken dark.

"Zane," Geoff hisses, clutching my forearm. Something booms, the house shudders. I shoot for the window, thinking tornado, lightning, guns. Light glows in the distance, bounces off windshields in the streets. Sirens wail from afar.

"What is it?"

"I don't know."

We stand, look at each other. Through the window we watch doors open, a woman in a housecoat emerge, a cat in her arms, the two of them trembling. Geoff takes my hand and we drift downstairs, brave, together, the smoke-sour air, the screaming night. Neighbours stand on their curbs—pointing, filming, all of them facing the same direction. Four blocks away, where our one-way street ends, a huge white cauldron blazes, mocks the dark.

"That's residential," Geoff says. "No big buildings down there."

The woman with the cat turns to us, her frayed house-coat shifting. "Explosion."

A crowd is thickening, drifting mothlike towards the white glow. There are families, teenagers, elderly couples, dog-walkers, cyclists. Most of them hold phones aloft, filming. I squeeze Geoff's hand. "Should we go look?"

"Come on," Geoff says. "Put a hoodie on." I almost laugh, then see Geoff's coiled, serious face as he grabs my wrist, tugs me along after him. He marches me through the house, filling water bottles, grabbing the bugout bags. Back in the driveway the white cauldron is rising in the distance, the horizon burning, smoke furling through the restless dark. Everyone is just standing, watching. We're thumping down-stairs past the whirling AC unit, climbing in the car and peeling out of the driveway, up Queen.

"Where are we going?"

"North."

The strange trembling light is in the rear-view mirror, an earthbound moon. Logically, I know it's foolish. I know Geoff is on an edge. I know that if there were real danger, everyone else would be getting in their cars too. But there is a large, real part of me that is genuinely terrified of that church-sized shuddering white flame.

Geoff roars the engine, turns up Adelaide. I turn the radio on, flip the channels. No news, just a talk show about barbecue pairings. We soar over the train tracks, head north, north. Past Arva and into the welcoming dark. The white flame still visible now and again in the rear-view, pulling me back to the sidewalk of my memory. What I see is cockroaches, clinging together against the flame. Roaches clambering, flailing, molten, sintered in the blaze.

"Geoff. This is terrifying."

"There's a place," he says. "I know a place. It's arranged already. We can go there until things cool down."

"What cools down?"

He stares at the road, curving over a distant hill.

"Geoff?"

"Just trust me."

He waves his hand towards the dark horizon. I skim through my phone, find nothing but speculation, a tweet from the police about a four-block evacuation radius, a fire crew, remain calm. I think about jumping, opening the door. Yellow lines splat by.

Instead, wearily, I slump into the leathery dark. I watch the rushing darkness lull by the window. Tobacco, soy, corn, mailboxes, tractors, the wending white line. I doze, wake, drooly, to the sound of Geoff peeing onto the shoulder. The road sign reads OWEN SOUND: 79. It's four in the morning. Geoff gets back in the car. I count the yellow stitches as they pass. Geoff drives on, tapping the dash.

In the dark distance the farms in the countryside are lush, summered. The road's shoulders wick and furl, furred with clover, chicory, knapweed. I look up through the sunroof, into the black. Satellites blink in a stubble of stars, and I think of the view from space. Take comfort knowing there is another vantage, a place where asphalt switchbacks swing calligraphic—a view that could render these ruins a rune.

Finally, the story comes on the news. We're deep in Huron County, an hour and a half from home. Geoff stops on the shoulder to listen. A natural gas explosion. A drunk driver—a teenager from Waterloo—had raced the wrong way up the street at reckless speed and ran head-on into a house, the car's hood and engine crumpling into a gas meter. The paramedics arrived within minutes, and, smelling the leaking gas, evacuated the residents. Fifteen minutes later, the explosion tore the roof off two houses. The white flame we had seen was gas. Pure gas, beaming upwards. Seven houses have been damaged but the situation is under control. There was a four-block radius evacuated, but the order was only precautionary.

"False alarm," Geoff says, slouched against the wheel.

Staring into the dark farms on the shoulders of the road, I think of pipelines, of the gas we call "natural." The enormous vulnerability of it. It almost seems a hoax.

Geoff turns to me in the dark, and I realize that cars driven at night share this intimacy with bedrooms. Faces, looking at each other in the dark. He rolls his window down and the smells of farms roll in. Grass, hay, irrigated earth. "Something's wrong," he says. Which I was not expecting.

"What?"

"I can feel it."

I nod, swallow. Between us the dark still and trembling.

"What do you need?"

All this time spent wanting to leave, and I am not prepared. A pair of headlights roll over a distant hill, sweep over the farms—a sea of waist-high soy. I tell him I need this to stop, I need him to have a job, I need to be happy, I need a future, I need to believe in some future, any future. I need strength for the present, to face this sick tired world. "I need you—here, now."

"Okay," he says. "All right."

Geoff pulls off the shoulder and turns the car around.

TWO HOURS LATER we come over the railroad bridge, beneath red trucks, the road lush with silent pulsing sirens. Pale light seeps over the breweries and abandoned factories, the rusted shopping carts under the bridge, goldenrod sprouting from a tossed truck tire. The road is closed so we park the car and walk. Drawing closer, we see the scorched roofs, the open beams, burnt chimneys. There's a pink three-wheeled scooter and a Paw Patrol helmet scorched on the front steps of one of the houses. A pillowcase caught under a blackened cinder block.

A few other people—a toothless man with a lapdog, a woman pushing a sleeping toddler—have also come to bear witness, to attest the wounded night. An excavator paws a burnt pit, coils of plumbing, clumps of melted shingle. A man with a hooked pole pulls scorched beams and warped furniture from the wreckage. Seven charred houses, four of them roofless, two totally demolished, the bare foundations full of flame-curled shingle, busted brick.

Holding Geoff and looking out at the ruined houses, what comes to mind is wildfire ecology, the controlled burn. An ancient practice, common across Indigenous cultures, as old as humanity. Healthy forests and grasslands maintain themselves with fire, and sometimes people need to imitate this process. Small, controlled fires can reduce the likelihood of serious, hotter, harmful blazes. In moderation, fire can help trees germinate, expose new mineral layers, and open tree cones to seeds. What a thing to contemplate: a world burning itself better, remaking in the ash.

"Are we all right?" Geoff says, taking my hand.

I tell him yes, we're all right. Because who would I be if I couldn't see by now that he was sick, scared, that his world had shuddered under him, revealed its sickly roots? That he needed help. We stand and stare into the burnt foundation. What's strange is the lawns. All of them intact. Grass, mulch, woolly thyme. Maple, sumac, black walnut. A flagstone pathway wending through bluestem, wide stone steps rising to a flame-razed doorway, the ghost of a home.

THE PIT

EDWARD IS NOT expecting her voice. "Why don't we go out?" They stand with their fingers in the pigeon mesh, the buildings on the far side lit sporadic, a zapped moth twitching in the wall sconce. Edward looks into Lily's riviera eyes, her pomegranate grin. Close and unseen, pigeons murmur and croon.

"Maybe not tonight," he says. "You know how it goes, how they see us."

Across Eglinton the buildings teeter, rock foot to foot in the wind. Lights blink on and off. He's always liked the randomness of apartment windows at night, the slapdash pattern of those square portals into other lives. TVs flicker, fridges open, a woman appears with a towel wrapped around her head.

"I want you to hold me," she says, looking off beyond the balcony. Below, far below, teenage trees bend yogic.

He steps close, sinks his chin into the nape of her neck. Drapes his arms around her, fingers linking over her navel.

Five years and here they stand at the brink of it. This world a tempest of flesh and lifespans.

Wind lashes the balcony, whorls city-grit on the concrete.

"Come on," he says. "We should go to bed. I need my beauty sleep."

She stares at him, mute. By the time she laughs it's not right anymore. He laughs back, sharp and mean. "Ha ha ha," he barks, sick with her, with himself.

THE FUNGUS DOES not itch, exactly, but radiates. The fungus pines for fingers, calls for the touch that will feed its spread. The fungus has eyes, stares back in dull mirrors. The fungus does not sleep. The fungus lies awake, glowing neon through the night.

It started as a dime-sized patch on his ankle. The doctor assured him it was nothing abnormal, likely contact dermatitis. She prescribed two creams, told Edward not to mix them. The fungus clambered on, vined up his calves, annexed his lower back. The fungus became a continent, then another. Slowly, the blobs became a Pangaea of rash. Now he wears long sleeves, rolls them up to scratch when no one is watching.

The fungus knows his dearest secrets, hears his dream-spilled longings, intuits his deepest want: to entice the hate in her, to taunt her to hurt, to shriek, to feel.

EDWARD TWIRLS THE pit, scrubs frying pans, cranks The Offspring over dishwasher hum. He brings out a stack of clean plates and sets them down on his side of the line. He avoids Seb's eyes. Seb who is thankfully occupied tonight, training the new cook, Owen. Seb whose title is kitchen manager though he calls himself sous-chef. Seb who got a totem pole tattooed on his calf when he found out his distant great-aunt was Lenape. Seb who once sent Edward a picture of his crooked engorged penis next to a wine bottle that turned out to be a novelty miniature airplane wine bottle. Seb who, last week, found out about Lily.

Sylvia, tonight's closer, comes in to pick up a dessert. When she spins off the line, Seb flails his hand near his groin, mimes a flamboyant spank. He sees Edward watching from the pit. Elaborates a wink. "Like that, Eddy?"

"What?"

Owen chuckles, snorts, pulls the element dials off to clean the steel underneath.

"You'd like to," Seb says. "Wouldn't you, Eddy? Real woman for a change?"

"Don't call me that."

Seb trades a look with Owen. "Sorry, Ed. Edmund?"

"Edward."

Seb snorts, keels over with his hands on his knees, cackling.

Edward turns up his music on the old grey CD player. He soaks the chafing dishes, the soup tureens. In his sink, heads of lettuce float, rinsing. A shallow pool in the cube of his spray-drain. Archipelagos of dining room gore. He plunges his drain and thinks about the debt, the repair bill, whether he could make it work.

He works slow and calm while the cooks close, sign out, lope down the back stairs. Out in the dining room, chairs are up on tables, the last guests gone. He pulls ice and lime from the well, tosses them into the blender with chunks of frozen mango. Sylvia passes by, spaghetti-string purse strung around her shoulder. She says good night and he says it back, but his voice is lost as he hits pulse on the blender, provokes a roar of ice and fruit, a shriek of bleeding green.

EDWARD DID NOT dream of this career, of doing shift work at fifty. But he'd trudged through school, didn't like the trades. Tried driving an asphalt truck and collecting debt over phones and found eventually that he liked the quiet, liked working nights, liked the gleam of clean glassware. He liked the rinse aid and detergent passing bright red and blue through their tubes. He liked coaxing an exodus of clung minestrone from the base of a tureen. He liked being alone in the pit, cleaning it piece by piece—plates, glassware, cookware—his small steel world slowly neatening. The final ritual of squeegeeing the counter, up to down, up to down, trying not to leave a streak and then standing back to behold his glimmering dominion of stainless steel. Sometimes at night, once he is finished, he turns the lights off, leans against the dishwasher, and runs it empty. Runs it just to run it, to hear it. Sits alone on the gleaming tiles listening to the thwump of water on the thin steel door, the squirm and churn of his chemical sea.

EDWARD'S CHILDHOOD is a nausea of KFC coupons, of listening for the phone to ring, staying home on Halloween tired of asking people to trick-or-treat with him. His father filling the room with Player's Light, shouting, "Fuck you're useless. You're a joke, a twat." His mother in curlers, spinning *Deal or No Deal*, spinning *Circus of Cash*. His childhood is boys with fingers in their mouths and the smell of fresh rain. Boys on a soccer field calling him Beaky, Bird-turd, Deadward. Sixth graders with basketball-smelling hands prying his mouth and shoving two fresh-dug worms in and he'd closed his lips and squirmed but he could not not taste them. Hands clamped over lips pressing down the taste of worm and blood the plastic smell of a basketball and he could not spit or bring himself to swallow so the worms went down on their own, slunk and wriggled into the earth of him where they wait, squirming, still.

GETTING OFF the streetcar, he sees a four-foot sapling growing out of a flaccid eavestrough, bloated with leaves. Is this flourishing or decay? The elevator is out again. Meaning walking up eighteen stories. Passing the thirteenth floor, fungus glowing under his pant leg, he thinks of the empty pool. The whole floor devoted to a pool that, due to an architectural miscalculation, could never be filled. The weight that would have tipped the balance of the building. He's always thought he would go in there, one day. Go alone, or take Lily. Sit at the bottom of the empty pool, in the guts of that oversight.

Lily sits at the table, smiling hard when he opens the door. He puts ramen in the microwave and changes into shorts. The doctor said it needs open air, does not like the wet. He sits at the table applying cream and telling her about the cooks, the towels, the jokes.

"Sounds like a pissing contest," she says, but she doesn't seem to remember Seb. It's getting worse and worse. She says she'd chalk it up to insecurity. He stares at his neglected weight bench, his stationary bike, his old Telecaster. She stays up with him for a while, watching some YouTube docs on alternative medicine. He tells her he hopes she doesn't mind but he might want to be alone tonight.

"Of course," she says. "Wake me if you need me."

She goes to bed and he scrolls electric. He plays *Overwatch*, plays *Assassin's Creed*, levels up. He plays *Life 2.0*, the game in which he is a dishwasher, but in the game he convinces Seb to reach a hand into the deep fryer.

Edward dreams a silken valley, lurid with reds and blues. The colour palette of a movie he'd watched as a boy. Rinse-aid blue, maraschino red. In the dream, they are on a neon toboggan, Lily close. They pass into a liquid moon, spend the day drinking piña coladas, toes spritzed in a lake of molten white.

He wakes, as usual, in the afternoon. Almost two. He's due at work at five. She lies beside him, her eyes fluttering locomotive. He finds that he's been scratching the fungus. It has spread again. It's on his left thigh, down his calf to the ankle. Red brittle, flaking. They shower together. He makes French press. It's a windy afternoon, and they stand in the living room, watch the buildings sway in the picture windows.

"Do you find it creepy?"

"Yes, a little. Do you?"

"Yes."

"Are you lying?"

"No. It's uncanny."

"They're supposed to do it. Absorbs the wind."

"You sound angry."

"I'm fine."

"Hold me."

IN THE PIT, lights slurring on the dark wet window, he changes the mophead, watches the chemicals slurp red and blue through their lines. He soaks the chafing dish, tries not to scratch. He turns towards the window, palms its cool. Gazes out at the scurrying couriers, the blinking cyclists, the dog-walkers stooping plastic-handed.

Sylvia appears, staring at the hose. Struck.

"What's wrong?"

"It's just—isn't it ridiculous? All that water? I mean the world's running out. Doesn't it just seem wasteful?"

Edward shrugs. "It's a living," he says.

"Order up," Seb calls from the line, and Sylvia trots off to collect a cheesecake.

The cooks sign out and he walks the kitchen alone. The yellowed tiles rimed with grease, the steel plateau of the flattop, the knives hung point-down from their magnets. Seb and Owen bark about the soap he left on the pans. He pours bleach into hot water, paints mophead S's on the tile.

He's preparing his smoothie when she appears, purse slung over her shoulder. In front of him, the blender's teeth seem to twinkle. "So," Sylvia says. "What are you watching lately?"

Sylvia knows about his YouTube sessions. Knows he considers himself an internet person, takes pride in that. He tells her about the alternative medicine doc, about maggot therapy, about biotherapy, about the Renaissance, the nineteenth century, a Confederate doctor in the Civil War. He tells her about diabetic ulcers, about rotten flesh. He tells her how it unnerves people to have creatures eat their wounded flesh, how they tend to think it's dirty but in fact the maggots are far more efficient, in terms of debridement, than surgery.

"Wow," she says, a glow in her eyes. "You're a neat guy, Edward."

He looks at her, hard, for a sign of pity, of condescension. She smiles, spins, gusts out the swinging doors.

HE GOES BACK to the walk-in clinic, shouts "fungus" to a receptionist who asks the reason for his visit. The doctor asks him stern questions, tells him not to scratch, prescribes an oral antifungal. He eats a sandwich, thinks about fermentation, about gut flora. The doctor says it might be necrotic. Maybe some kind of flesh-eating virus. Hard to say. The doctor prescribes antibiotics. "We'll monitor. See how you respond."

At work he watches the sun go hazy on the windows. He runs the dishwasher just to hear it. Stares at the clear tubes pumping hydroxide red and rinse-aid blue. The machine, his square companion, slurping thirstily. Sylvia comes and goes, does not ask about documentaries. He thinks of bread, of blue cheese, various accidents of rot. He thinks about Lily, his irrational rage, wonders how he can deal with it, whether he should.

When he goes downstairs to change the rinse aid, he finds a thick tail curling out from under the cans of tomatoes. The least pleasant part of his job. He wraps the plastic bag, turns his face away, and reaches in. He imagines it squirming, thrashing. He pictures the bald patch on its shoulder, louse-gnawed. He gags as he hefts it, turns it over, tail noodling out of the sack.

Coming back upstairs, he hears Seb's gritty frog voice talking loud, laughing. He stops, around the corner, rat parcel in his hands. He can hear that Seb is at the bar. The dining room must have emptied. He hears Seb say "girlfriend," say "sicko." He hears someone laughing. Seb saying "debt," saying "hemorrhage," saying "those things cost fifty grand."

"He's a robojohn!" This must be Owen's voice.

Seb goes tin-can monotone: "Oh Eddy, Eddy, please have your way with me."

He thinks about skulking off. He could still go without being seen. But he's not leaving, not moving. He's standing still.

Edward emerges, then. Walks around the corner and sees them. As expected, Owen and Seb, smiling dumbly. But, then, there is Sylvia. Seb's arm around her, chuckling, smiling, happy, included. And Edward finds himself foolish, courageous with rage. The three so quiet. An acoustic version of "Don't Stop Believin'."

Seb stares, snickers. Peels his arm off Sylvia and steps forward. Grins too hard: "Hi Eddy."

Edward doesn't say anything. Sylvia's eyes are pinned to the floor.

"Is there a problem?" Seb says, smile gone.

In his hand, the plastic trembles. He feels the weight of the rat, thinks its dead eyes. He steps closer. In his mouth the taste of distant soil. Of fingers, of blood.

"What are you going to do, Eddy?"

Edward walks up to Seb and drops the rat at his feet, where it lands with a wet thud. A paw slinks out of its Loblaws body bag as Edward spins, walks through the swinging doors.

THE GENUFLESH XS-4000 is a fully customizable intimacy model, with self-lubricating genitals and modifiable vocabulary. The GenuFlesh XS-4000 contains a self-moulding labial apparatus that forms in complement with the organs of its primary user. The compatibility option allows GenuFlesh anthropomorphic robobrides to sense and respond to pheromones. The chameleoskin feature tracks temperature, senses mood changes, and reflects arousal as signalled. Premium models are free-standing with customizable voices and responsive touch. Convivial chips enable intimacy models to quote poetry, share opinions on news, history, and politics, and to respond affably and organically to user-shared information and life events.

HE PASSES THE NIGHT in cold rage. He eats spaghetti, lies in bed twitching, unable to sleep. The fungus swells, pulses, grows tentacles. The fungus crawls onto his tongue. She comes awake, asks how he's feeling, if he's all right, if she should call a physician. He says no, gets up.

"Do you want some company?"

"I want to be alone."

"Do you want some company?"

"No. I don't know."

"Hold me."

"No thank you."

"Hold me."

He screams to the ceiling: "I fucking need to be alone."

"All right," she says. "All right. Fine."

HE DREAMS HIMSELF in a red and throbbing wetsuit on the roof of the building. It's hot, and black, a bitumen roof and it's dark out, the windows of all the neighbouring buildings flashing on and off. There are trees climbing up the sides of the building, trees with long roots like tentacles, branches like gnarled clawed rat paws. Trees that crowd around him, long fingers plucking tremolo at his pant legs, the fungal patches on his elbow. Trees that jeer, prod. Spiky branches and grume of soil and their long, kinked fingers clawing at his mouth, root-feet pushing him down into the bitumen roof that has become a kind of trench, cool and earthen. The trees hunched scatter-limbed and their reedy wind-voices saying look at him, saying pathetic, saying this one deserves to rot.

HE GETS UP and takes a cold shower. He stares at *Life 2.0*, imagines himself burning the game-restaurant to the ground. He eats a mountain of Corn Flakes, then a mountain of Lucky Charms. He searches his phone, then computer, for the miniature wine bottle picture. Lily offers sex and he finds himself curling into her, giving in to a deep dry sob. Finds himself holding her, gripping, heaving, gasping.

"Let's go out," she says. "Take me dancing."

Night stalks the window. "Sure," he says. "Fine."

On the streetcar, he puts his arm around her. A woman with a headscarf and a rolling grocery cart glares at them, fixates on Lily's breasts. Edward smiles at her and says hello. They find a karaoke bar full of sauced bluehairs in scooters. He gets them each a dark and stormy then takes her out on the dance floor and spins long and slow as a peroxide starlet croons "Love Me Tender." They spin and spin, her body holding the heat of his. Their chests gumming together and she is smiling her stiff pert grin, the men and women looking on curious, shrewd. The bar filled with the smell of talcum and stale beer and the sour amalgam of spilled liquor stomped into bar mats. Above them the woeful silver planet slings its pinata of stars, disco ball light dapples her face and though her feet aren't moving he can almost forget the difference between flesh and made.

What he cannot almost forget is the old man in the cowboy hat, beer quivering, dentures grinding. Or the young gun, the sixty-something in bowling shirt, handlebar moustache and a charlatan nest of too-black hair.

"Get out of here," someone says.

"It's not right."

"Pervert."

"Sicko."

Someone shoves him and he's gasping, tumbling. He drops her and her head thwacks off the floor and the gathered crowd is laughing and jeering. Edward kneels down, the lights slumping over him, over her. The disco ball still spinning as the song ends. Silver dollars whirling over her face, their limbs, the revolving wash of floor.

SHE IS BREAKING down and he cannot afford the repairs and his mind is a corrosion of worry, a tinnitus of hurt. She is breaking down because she, too, is a body. Petroleum-derived—silicone, polypropylene, semiconductors, integrated circuits—but body still, matter still. She is breaking down because these things are metal and oil heated and catalyzed and elaborately moulded. Because she lives in the limn, a world made flesh.

NO ONE SEES him drag her into the restaurant as they are closing for the night. No one sees him take her out to the empty dining room, open the blender in the stark light of the bar.

"Goodbye," he says.

"Goodbye," she says back.

"Do you understand? Fuck. Of course not."

The plan is never to hurt her because how could he? The plan is not to get mad. The plan is to blend, to disperse, to end the sham. The plan is the blender roaring, rearing, whirring, the blade spinning like a deranged steel petal. He powers the machine on, raises Lily to a sitting position on the bar and cups her face in his hands.

"Hey," Sylvia says, stepping forward through the swinging doors. She eyes him hard. Behind her the doors whine and flap, send a gust through her hair.

"Sorry," he falters. "I thought I was alone."

Sylvia looks hard at Lily. Comes close. He shudders, flinches. "It's all right," she says, staring at Lily. "It's fine. I think it's cool. Whatever."

"Cool?" Edward laughs. He can see that Sylvia is struggling.

"And I'm sorry about the other night. I should have said something. Those guys are pricks. Seb's still mad about the wine bottle photo."

"Here," she says, reaching into her purse. "I was going to wait for tomorrow. But I got you a present."

She produces a small plastic jar with an orange lid. He takes it, holds it. Inside, there's a little zip-lock pouch full of tiny yellow worms.

"Larvae," she says. "Green bottle fly. Turns out it's a trend in alternative medicine. FDA approved. Just a joke, but, well."

"Thank you," he says. Something strange roils through his insides. Something soft and clear. "Thank you," he says again.

HIS CHILDHOOD is a nausea of smokewash and worm-mouth until it becomes something else, a squishy torture. A girl a year younger, blond with a snout nose, and her friends are saying she likes you, saying ask her to the dance, and he is pawing the phone book and finding her mother, speaking gutclutched to her parents and then she's on the line, saying yes with a giggle. A giggle that turns out to mean feigning sweetness, walking with him arm in arm and asking if he wants to get hot chocolate on the way. Hot chocolate that turns out to be laced with copious Ex-Lax. Meaning all of grade nine laughing outside the bathroom. Meaning photos of his feet under the toilet stalls and this would set the tenor of his love life. Three dates in high school, gradually lowered standards and increasing desperation in his early twenties until he found himself alone at a forestry camp at thirty. Alone in the bush with his laptop paying women to talk to him, women in Colombia and Hungary and Arizona, women with cupboards full of wands and beads and suction toys listening solemn telling him he was worthy, telling him he was a good sweet man as he keeled over and wept to the laptop slicing blue through Selkirk dark.

AT HOME HE POWERS her on, puts her in platonic mode, and tells her he's sorry, she doesn't deserve this, any of it. He tells her it's been hard for him but he knows he should do better, can do better. She asks what he needs, and he says nothing. She says she's tired, asks what time it is. Bedtime, he tells her. Gentle, he touches her neck, reaches for the switch behind her hair. Gentle, he shuts her down. Gentle, he takes her in his arms, drags her across the carpet, the laminate, sets her in the closet. Kisses her soft before closing the door.

Through the darkness, they find the fungus almost instantly. Their rough tickle a chorus of coarse and tender tongues. He lies on the bed, staring out the window where the buildings lean and sway in a gathering storm. He does not sleep, not quite, but recedes into a deeper calm. The maggots swarm the rash, spread and skitter, a perfect smothering. The skin calms, cools, almost purrs. Far below, trees stoop and swish, bend to nearly touch the street, the roofs of parked cars. The city trees, concrete-footed, their roots distant though they would like to mingle, to touch, entangle. Maggots cool as menthol, soft as down. The larvae feed, nibble, writhe and squirm and devour him free.

DREAM HAVEN

I CINCH THE tourniquet around the flub of Jane's biceps while she tells me about human waste, ninety-two years of excrement, the mass of it. The sky-blue sash parts the cellu-lite sea of Jane's upper arm and she asks me to picture it: a landfill of shit, piss, puke, semen, blood. Four children, a husband who put a clothespin on his nose to change a diaper when she was in the hospital for mono. "Four kids," she says. "Think of the volume. The sheer volume." She clucks, looks me brow to toe. "Always cloth, of course. But what would you know about kids?" She grins hard. "Pretty young thing like you."

"Right," I say, clenching the wound of me: "Now make a fist."

Jane does, and I sink the needle in—not mean, but firm. She's got small veins, her grey skin blotched, loose, reticent. Blood flushes into the vial. Jane winces, watching her blood accumulate in the glass chamber. There's a mouldy smell in the room, like someone forgot to clean the mophead. Which is better than urine or *C. diff* or UTI.

On Jane's windowsill, three parched houseplants bend for the sun, along with her daily Sudoku regimen, her botany textbooks, her volumes of Nabokov, Woolf, Neruda. "The brain is a muscle," she said once. "Needs flexing." Outside, lawn mowers buzz down the long hill in front of the DREAM HAVEN sign.

As I'm sliding her sample into my case, Jane grabs my hand. "Don't go," she says. She swallows, wiggles her dentures. Retracts her thin lips. "For five years," she says, "I've gone to bed every night hoping to die." She pauses, swallows, breathes. "You can't know what it's like until you're here. You can't imagine cataracts, arthritis, the falls, the fear, the brittle bones, the bruises, the pneumonia, pressure sores up your hips, buttocks, feet." She clucks. "Bless my dainties: Pain each way you turn."

She pauses, stares at the model sailboat on her dresser. "I've wanted so much to die," she says, one shaky hand warding around her small room, the other still locked on my wrist. "But not like this. Never like this."

Jane does not need to say "virus." She does not need to cite her desperation, say that she can't see her family, that she's lonely, scared as the rest of them. She does not need to mention her neighbour, Martha, who broke a rib coughing last week. Martha who was carted to St. Joseph's yesterday, declared dead this morning.

"It's all right," I tell her. "We'll do our best."

She nods, releases my wrist. "Of course."

In the nursing station, I set Jane's sample in the LifeLabs cooler then pause, beholding the neat rows of carefully labelled human blood. The essence of life, itemized. I think of the volume, all the blood I have pumped out of people. I wonder what happens to it, after testing. Where is it dumped? I think of vats of the stuff, blood types slurping together. Crimson icebergs in a surging sea.

WHAT JANE DOESN'T know because how could she is that you are not a pretty young thing, are in fact thirty-eight and have always looked young with your downy round cheeks and Maeby Fünke freckles. What she does not know is that you may not know children of your own but you do know geriatric IVF pregnancy. What she does not know is temperature monitoring, FSH, estradiol. The moment when sex becomes "trying." The moment when "trying" becomes failing. When the doctors won't even look at you for a year and after that it's ruling the obstacles out one item at a time. Ryan's motility technically fine but on the low side. One doctor calling his semen "lethargic." What Jane does not know is the moment when trying becomes needing, fiending, ravening for child. The whole time Ryan smiling when needed, hugging when needed, giving space when required, understanding if you weren't up to it that night. What Jane doesn't know is two years along joining an online support group that turns out to be strangely Christian. An online support group where women have names like "Mom2Be" and "Praying4babies" but these women become closer than your former friends who shrink away from your talk of anti-Müllerian, fertility charts. These online voices become your anonymous disciples, sing your body in their mantras: "your womb is an orchard," "you are not a desert," "own your cycles." Words that live and throb in the seas of you. Words you hold tender as children. Words that would have rung different before this but now you are desperate for something like faith. What Jane does not know is implantation, the two-week wait, the radiance of the word "viable." You and Ryan stupidly agreeing that you liked the name "Sacha" for either sex and then a torture you could never have conjured. The news broken on the television—your doctor an architect of elaborate violation. Such fairy-tale malice could not be you, never you. Absolutely could not be you, and unquestionably was.

RYAN LOOKS UP from his laptop, pops an earbud out, head bobbing to the beat. He's onto his chapter on British rap— you can hear the accent. For two weeks he's been trying to decide if he should mention his race, if it'll count against him or not. "Always seems to," he said.

He's working on a funding application for his thesis on the poetics of hip-hop lyrics. On his lap, a "Decomposition Book" where he measures the scansion, the metre, the intricate towers of stacked rhymes. Beside him a Jenga of books: *The Sound Studies Reader, The Anthology of Rap, They Can't Kill Us Until They Kill Us*. He asks how was work today and I tell him the usual, plod to the bedroom for pyjamas. You learn quick what you can and can't share, what loved ones can hear but not compute.

Back in the living room, hair in a topknot, scrubs in the laundry bin, I tell him three new cases, no new deaths. He says it's all bullshit. I ask what he means and he says all of it: the funding application, the experience of sitting on every diversity committee because he's the only Black person in the program. He folds his laptop closed, stands and walks to the front window, easing into his thinking face as he tells me about the latest email from his supervisor. His painfully woke supervisor who keeps recommending that he do a "genealogy" of Freudian themes from Langston Hughes to Tupac Shakur, who keeps offering fascinating connections between rap and what he calls "real" poetry.

"They love to stick me on the committee but when it comes to the work they're happy to belittle, to engineer, to tell me what's art, what's real. If I was a white guy studying hip-hop I'd be radical. I'd be sexy. Flash and panache."

I nod, take his hand. Sometimes there's nothing to do but listen, admit I can't know. He clucks, sets his hands on his temples. "There's more Black boys writing poetry in the streets than toting guns. But what they're doing isn't 'real.'"

We go outside, sit drinking licorice tea. I stare into the old koi pond, the sludge of dead leaves and algae. Ryan kneels in the garden, plucks weeds from his sagging tomato beds. The pond was here when we took the house, splurging on three-bedroom rent back when we thought a child was imminent. We figured the pond would be a death trap, so we told the landlord we'd tear it down. Now here we are, three years later, and agreeing to tear it down means not changing the filters or pumping the water or cleaning out that 7-Eleven Big Gulp container that drifted over the fence last fall. When friends used to come visit, I'd tell them our side business was a hobby mosquito farm.

I watch the petals floating in the pond, the ivy clambering haywire behind it. "Can you please do something about this mess?"

"The pit of despair?" Our private joke, long since unfunny. The things we cling to, say just to say. "Is it my job?" Ryan flashes his strong white teeth. "Isn't that a bit gender normative?"

I don't say "home all day." I don't say "word count." I don't say "thumb up your ass." Technically, nothing's changed for Ryan since the virus. He's still writing his dissertation, living in his own mind, searching Spotify lists and reading articles about the culture industry's refusal to acknowledge Black art. Ryan has worked at home for three years to achieve his word count, which he calls an "arduously researched zero."

"I'm getting to it," he says, chuckling to himself. "Trust me, I'm ruminating on it." A mosquito lands on my arm and I grind it dead. A pair of starlings shakes the canopy of the black walnut. We pause to watch them climb the greying sky.

Ryan turns to me, abruptly serious: "You know it's been three years."

I nod. "Last week."

He breathes deep, stares at the carriage lane, the parking space peppered with black walnut balls. Behind him the leaning fence, the parched grass, the raccoon-pawed compost bin. "I was thinking we could try." He swallows. Reaches down to scratch a bite on his leg. "Again. Start trying."

I wave around the yard, the sky. Invisible menace in a flapping hand. "You really think it's a good time to start anything?"

"Sure," he says, pinching a mosquito between thumb and forefinger. "Why not?"

Sufficiently bitten, we head inside, lie sleepless in the May heat, listen to the raccoons stalk the roof, the squirrels scrabble in the porch. A storm builds but doesn't break. In the attic, something groans.

IN THE DREAMS he is bald, slick, Picard-esque, the world behind him stainless steel. In the dreams his teeth are a flawless universe of white as he smiles his irked bureaucrat smile. His hands pellucid, each finger a gleaming needle. In the dreams there are glimmering steel shelves. Shelves and plates and in those petri dishes I can see tiny bodies, red bodies with hundreds of furling filament limbs. In the dreams he produces whitening strips from his pockets and lays them gently on my teeth. In the dreams Ryan hovers in a corner, watching mute and slack. In the dreams Dr. Spencer puts his needled hands on mine, finger to finger. "Here is the church, and here is the steeple." In the dreams his mandible fingers crawl my belly, slow. In the dreams he has a pig's tail, rising behind him curlicued and neon, floating as if animate. In the dreams Dr. Spencer's voice is thick and sharp as sanitizer as he leans in, brushes my cheek with his needle fingers, tells me I won't feel a thing.

IN THE MORNING I walk to work, pass the basketball courts strung with drooping yellow caution tape, the same tape that belts the swing sets like a father's Christmas wrapping job. A hive of gutter-flung masks, elastics coiled and tangled. A frat boy's panty trove. I walk through Victoria Park, buzzing with the ghosts of last year's cyclists and skate-boarders, of Ribfest and Jazzfest and Folkfest. Others walk alone or in pairs, step aside politely or don't. A whole new array of manners, of offences. I skirt the graveyard I used to walk through. It has rained, and the smell of fed soil pumps up from the river, flirts over the grass. Between the plots, the grass is rising fast and ragged. There's a frilled silvery-white lichen that grows on the older headstones. A fringed thing—round, blotched, imperfect saucers, the metallic shade never quite the same. In second-year biology I learned that lichen are fungal composites, a mixture of fungi and bacteria. Life, persistent life, growing across these gravestones.

Post-virus, Dream Haven is poised, sapped, quiet. Last summer, when I arrived for an evening shift, Linda would be out front perched in her Ventura, strumming Nancy Sinatra tunes on her ukulele while the card players spat and swore and warned passersby not to drop their dog-poop bags in the centre's garbage bin.

Death has been gentle, here, but fear has not. There are more protocols, fewer breaks, less training, fewer supplies. The food is still good, but the guests can't mingle; they've been divided, somewhat arbitrarily, into "friendship pods." Ala, who was the events coordinator, has basically become the manager of social distancing. Where once there was flirting, ballroom dancing, bingo, there is now proper hand-washing training, a single "bubble buddy," dining room pods, arrows sketched out in tape to indicate walking lanes. My work is fundamentally the same: care plans, call bells, interventions, purposeful hourly rounding. Daily, I remind myself that I am lucky to work at a boutique facility with fifty-six residents and two full-time security guards.

Today, I clean my hands raw, lather them in Vaseline, collect the anteroom bag, drugs, arterial line, and central venous catheter. Then I don my PPE and head to the 100s to see our four active cases. I check the filters, the charts, the reports, the stock, make sure the labels are right and the ventilators are clean. First, the 100s. Last week Rhonda had to send out a disciplinary memo after she'd heard the staff were calling this floor "Death Row." 101: temperature normalizing. 102: stabilizing. 103: cough, fever, signs of delirium. 104: not responding to oxygen administered via nasal prongs. Request ambulance and oversee transfer to hospital.

Break is a muffin, some emails, Rhonda's memos, texting my mother to assure her it's still safe to work, that this is not New York. Afterwards, I head up to the 200s, work through the urgents, the moderates, the milds. 201: pressure ulcers, mild fever, requisition for COVID-19 swab. 202: incontinence, UTI, routine requisition. 203: paraplegic, under-rotated. Requisition for physical therapy. 204: vital sign checks, medication checks, requisition for COVID-19 swab. 205: administer medications, intravenous therapy, wound care.

The 300s is called, with loving irony, the condom floor. The 300s is the salsa lessons floor, the tiara floor, the dating floor, the floor full of dye jobs and snuck cans of tonic, mickeys of Courvoisier. It's called the condom floor because when I suggest contraception after freezing off their warts or giving them antibiotics for discharge, they wince and recoil as if I've said a dirty word. Usually, I have little reason to go to the 300s, but lately I've been going up just to walk the halls, to hear the laughter, to watch them joke and hold their thumbs over FaceTime cameras, to hear them getting skunked and shooting moons.

The tests come back: no new cases today. I wash my face shield, order the new PPE though none of it is coming. Rhonda sends a memo to all staff, asking that in spite of everything the PSWs keep turning the bodies, turning the bodies.

RYAN WAS MAKING bad Duomom jokes when we found out. Having just learned that the implantation had gone well, we were sitting in the living room giddy with viability. The TV on silent in the background as we sat on the stained couch, our feet on the frayed rugs, all of which I realized we'd need to replace if we were to become parents. Above us, the ceiling fan spun. We talked about the oocytes, my brood, the seven that had been viable, the two they'd transferred, the five others we'd cryopreserved. I joked about having finally emerged from the cleavage stage. Ryan asked if we could have had all seven if we'd wanted, then started talking about Octomom. I didn't know Octomom but I saw her as a kind of sea creature: bioluminescent, floating in the midnight zone, each limb a gestating child. Ryan said maybe Duomom would be more accurate, then laughed hard at his own joke.

Through this bruised bliss watching the screen where I saw tanks in Venezuela. A dust storm in Texas. The Mexican president announcing a border gathering in honour of national dignity. The Department of Energy re-branding exports as "freedom gas." Shakira testifying about tax evasion before a court in Spain. A crack in the aquarium, the woes of the world spilling in. And then the thing that could not be possible, the thing you do not hear or rather read about on the news. Just words running along the bottom while above someone speaks at an unrelated press conference.

Fertility clinic foul play.

Just words and the name that must have been a different Dr. Spencer, a quantity of women that could not be real. It passed too fast to be real and this could not be the way to learn such a thing. Only then my phone buzzing in my pocket. Only then noticing three missed calls. The story was gone, had left the screen, and I hoped it would never come back and then it did.

In vitro scandal.

Over sixty women injected.

Ryan staring at the screen, mouth slack. Ryan reaching out as if to take my hand, unable to pull his eyes from the screen, missing my hand and sort of pawing the air. Ryan not moving, his face paling. On my phone: a voice mail from a detective wanting a statement. An urgent email from the clinic. I rose, stumbling, walked outside into the sun-shook world knowing it could not have been me, could not have been us and was. Somewhere a car alarm bleated, bleated, bled.

JANE IS STARING at the orange-vested man riding the lawn mower down the long hill as I unpack the specimen-collection kit. "Are you worried?"

"No. It's routine." I hand her a tissue. "Blow, please."

A man in orange headphones roars a string trimmer around the edges of the long sloping lawn. Neat, wide stripes. Stadium stripes. The lawn people see from the busy road on the way to the mall. A geriatric Hollywood crowned with a billboard of two smiling whitehairs and the caption: DREAM HAVEN: AGE IN STYLE.

I check for obstructions, then reach for the swab as Jane tells me about forest bathing. Her grandson has sent her an article. "He's a good kid," she says. Then, matter-of-factly: "Though he is a homosexual." I swallow, mine my mind for care. Jane tells me forest bathing is not what you think; it's not like a big bathtub in a sea of ferns. It's not a pine needle smoothie or a hot tub in the canopy or a moss hammam. "You just stand there," Jane tells me. "You look at trees." She works her dentures. "Good for the nervous system. The article said it was the"—she pauses, feels out the word— "parasympathetic."

She beams, repeats: "Parasympathetic."

I tell her to lean back and open her mouth. As I swab around her tonsils and pharynx, what lingers in my mind is liquid forest. A forest run through a blender. Pulped green and brown, the fragrance of liquefied humus, leaf, fern, moss, pine. I picture gravestones lost to lichen, crumbling in a gigantic mortar, the unmowed graveyard grasses rising, seeding, a green rain pouring down, chubby fingers doodling on the steamed glass walls, steam hazing the clumped roots of fallen trees, the earth soupy, swampy, a mire of rock and forest and body, bubbling and stewing together, churning, sweating, the intoxicate smell of earth and rot, spore and seed, Big Gulps, Matcha Monsoons, pits of despair.

As I pull the swab out and slide it into the Universal Transport Medium, Jane says the problem is she's not terminal.

"What do you mean?"

She breathes, rasping.

"Otherwise I could have MAID. 'Medical assistance in dying.' They won't say what it really is, of course." She rolls her eyes. "Death by euphemism."

I snort, not sure if I should let the laugh come through. I stand, set the vial in my case. Jane looks at me for a long time, measuring. I meet her gaze and hold it, feel the rhythm of her need. Her eyes are pale, fierce, almost colourless, the edges hazy with cataract.

"Terminal," she says, as if the word were cure.

WHAT YOU ARE not taught at nursing school is the smell of C. diff, of UTI, of death. What you learn fast and hard is that the body is a swampy thing. You learn that there is no sickness and health; there is pain and management, care plans and shades of decay. Flesh must be handled delicately, creams applied in the right ratio, limbs turned, given air and sun. What you are not prepared for is code white, restless anger, an in-patient in your practicum reaching into her stoma and tugging up a clutch of feces to hurl at the staff nurse. The smell of burnt flesh. A man in your emergency practicum with an abscess on his jugular from injecting crack. What you are not prepared for is sundowning, the staff overusing the restraints—physical, chemical, environmental. The staff "misplacing" guests' walkers so they don't have to deal with them moving and what you are not prepared for is getting that, knowing full well why. Sabine in 302 phoning her long-dead parents, phoning her brother over and over, telling him to get home quick, screaming out about a nightmare, lobsters in the bathtub: "They're in the tub, they're in the tub, get them off me, get them off me." Alice ringing her bell in the pitch of night. Shrieking out, caterwauling, call bell dinging, dinging, her harried screaming waking everyone on the floor and when you get there she's patting the mattress, telling you she can't find her TV remote. What you are not prepared for is declaring a man dead then walking into the next room to a guest asking where you've been, why didn't you bring the blanket she'd asked for? A woman with bald patches and fungal scalp and oozy caramel eyes telling you she needs water, she needs her family, she needs care. His last sour sweat still thick on your neck and this woman needing her blanket. These are the things you tell your nurse friends but not your partner because how could he get what it means to leave one room, one rotten clinging life, and walk into the next?

AT HOME, HEADPHONES on, Ryan leans over the man-scrawled wilderness of his notepad. Deep in what he calls his "idea factory," he mouths "five minutes." I get changed and cruise the iPad, wind up reading about milk, the milk people are no longer buying, the middlemen shutting down business and the supply chain slowing so the farmers are dumping milk into fields. Milk slurring into muck at the back ends of pastures where cattle are already injected with diuretics so their poop can be hosed off the platform.

When I approach, Ryan orbits his "idea factory" finger again so I go down to the basement to put my scrubs in the laundry. In the mouldy basement there are huge spider-webs, crumbling concrete stairs, a back section I don't even allow myself to think about, an old washer and dryer left by the previous owners. I manage the laundry in, fan some cobwebs, try not to think about Jane's dentures, her house-plants, the fear in her shaking wrists.

My mother calls wanting to know about elder abuse, about the horror show. She has read the articles, knows about the poor pay, the lack of protection for the workers, the man who was supposed to feed patients by hand but just left hours-late food outside their doors. The nurse in Quebec who walked into a care home and found it desolate, devoid of support workers, the guests groaning and leaking, coughing and soaked, wheezing and helpless, alone. The article about the nurse who went to the beds one by one, who changed the fluids and turned the bodies and declared the dead.

"It's not like that, Mum. That's not me."

"What's it like then?"

"I'm sure that stuff goes on, but I don't see it. Dream Haven is a boutique facility."

"Privatization. That just means they can pay the staff less."

"It's bad, it's hard. What do you want me to say?"

"It's Quebec," she says. "I'm sure it's mostly Quebec."

Ryan is still slumped into his laptop, typing now. He unplugs his headphones, asks again if he thinks he should disclose his race for the funding application. Or would it be too stereotypical? Give them a chance to profile him?

I tell him I don't know, I honestly don't. When we were pregnant, we had a similar conversation. "You're going to have a Black kid," he said. "You're going to have to figure it out." It hurt, and I tried to let it, to hold the pain close, to feel my small portion of a dominion of pain.

Now, I stand staring at our houseplants, the kitchen, the worn yellow linoleum with the burn mark in the shape of a bird, the old fridge humming loud. I wonder what Jane would think of me and Ryan having children. I've mentioned Ryan often, but never mentioned his race. I think of Dr. Spencer, how although he did it to sixty-one other women maybe he particularly liked whitening my child.

Ryan slaps his laptop closed. Rises and suggests a walk. We stride past the cathedrals, past the seminary, turn down to the river towards the sinking sun. Willows, goldenrod, spring blossoms, goose shit. The sun lowering, tufts of yellow catkins twirling through the air. People wearing masks, gloves, walking too close, stepping far wide of us. We climb a footbridge, stand looking over the river as it rushes towards the parched city of stuck trees. At the bank of the river, there's a length of eavestrough, a rusted toaster, a Styrofoam coffin crumbling in the clay.

"I know it's been a lot," Ryan says.

"What?"

"Everything."

Below us, a broken tree limb slumps down the river.

"I think I've only just managed to believe it," he says, and I realize he's not talking about the virus or my work but about Dr. Spencer, the implantation. I watch two mallards chasing a pale brown female in the slurred yolk of the lowering sun and Ryan says contamination. He says he sees now that it was always about contamination. The river blurs and races beneath us, toting sticks and feathers and a water-bloated dog-poop bag and Ryan is saying that maybe contamination can be good, productive. Maybe art can be a kind of contamination, maybe his thesis can contaminate the canon. He's talking about Fanon, about combat literature, how art always emerges in moments of upheaval. He's talking about jazz and blues and who cares if the master won't admit when his house is burning.

I nod, smile, tell him that he's sexy, beautiful. I tell him that he's right, that I want to audit his classes someday. Below us, the ducks keep riding the current and what else could they be doing but playing? Hustling and charging against the river's weight then circling in the eddy and riding it back, earnest oblivions. How nice it would be not to know the virus was out there, somewhere, riding breath and spit and fingertips.

Ryan looks at me like he wants to say something else. Like he wants to say the obvious. I think of what it means to try trying again. But he knows what I'll say, he knows I'm tired, worn, mowed by time and care.

We turn back, darkness thickening, a chubby spandexed cyclist whizzing past. Needing a cushion against the unsaid, I tell Ryan about forest bathing, about Jane, about the nervous system. He listens hard, watching his feet pass over the trail. "Para what?"

"Parasympathetic."

He smiles, half to himself. I ask what and he says, "The etymology. It means 'beside care.'" So rarely, these days, does Ryan give the response I'm looking for. There are no lights down here by the river, so the darkness comes full and sudden. The air changes, soured by a distant skunk. And then, all at once, the fireflies emerge. A festival of beetle-borne light. Ryan grabs my hand and we pause, there, without needing to speak. Holding together as those minute cauldrons flicker and vanish, shudder and pulse.

HOW DO YOU cope with a thing like that? An IVF maniac injecting you and sixty-one other women with his sperm. You don't cope. You join a chat group called Dr. Spencer Survivors, listen to the women debating, the women saying it's their fault, saying it's their last chance, they're thinking about keeping it. The women who were further along than you, who were already calling it "baby." The women reaching term, the women with three-year-old children, none of them knowing for sure if he tampered or if maybe it was all a lie. The women saying we are a family, saying we were all brought to this crisis together.

You stare into the showerhead thinking about embryos, about agar plates, about the cryogenically frozen viable leftovers. You remember when Ryan called the chat group "TERF-y," how you told him he didn't get it but mostly what you thought of was turf. The Astroturf steps of your grandfather's home, walking on it and thinking that must be what it felt like to walk on the moon. You remember finding out what TERF meant, feeling sick with Ryan and his quick judgments, his knee-jerk politics, his positions that always, in the end, turned out to be thoughtful, informed, right.

How do you cope? You curse Ryan, you slam doors, you rage at Ryan when he leaves the clothes drying in the rain or buys the toilet paper you hate. You swell sour with rage seeing pregnant women on the streets. You call your mother and can't tell her, can't possibly tell her. You ask Ryan to tell her, get enraged because he does it over text. You take leave from work. You go for a run and find yourself on the side of the highway, looking over a river where someone has dropped an old fridge into the water. The corpse of it lying there busted, strewn. Half a produce shelf full of twigs, leaf, rock while the current scrubs it clean, coaxes its plastic shards gradually to the ocean, a continent away. You lie on your back and stare at the pocked ceiling panels as the slim blond doctor injects the anaesthetic and tells you to breathe. You lie there clenching as the vacuum purrs, knowing nothing could numb you, knowing there are things you cannot terminate.

THE SHIFT BEGINS with a meeting and a training session on the dispersion factor, then a video on oxygen therapy and intubation thresholds. After that Rhonda asks me to train new staff on the second floor. In 306 there's a new patient with a badly neglected pressure sore on his heel and ankle. The entire area purple, almost black. The wound cratered. Rhonda asks if I mind demonstrating. I tell her no, slip the gloves on. The patient is diabetic, not ambulatory, staring at the ceiling, clearly used to interventions. Rhonda explains about cell death, about wound care, about ischemic necrosis. I tell the new workers that this is not their job, of course, but it's good for them to see it because this type of ulcer is unacceptable. We need to take preventative measures: special pillows, mattress pads, powder, dressings, keep the patients walking, moving. Turn the bodies, always turn the bodies. Rhonda passes me the saline solution and I rinse the wound, gentle the flesh loose. Chunks of violet skin flaking off, globs of body fat. I reach a gloved finger into the crater, explaining to the staff that this one may need a requisition for surgical debridement. The smell of wound thickens through the room as I dig my index in, feel something brittle against my finger. The patient shifts a little, and I assure the trainees he can't feel this. The trainees stand and stare as I reach in, pinching, pulling out a shard, a thumb-sized flake of human bone.

JANE IS TELLING me about her girlhood cat. "Zola." She grins. I've finished explaining the results of her bloodwork and how we're still waiting on the swab. But she's asked me to stay a moment and now is telling me about the cat that used to climb from the roof into her window, used to set maimed sparrows at the foot of her bed but finally got old, started refusing the litter box, her coat gone patchy, flea-gnawed. The cat who'd been pregnant once but only gave birth to one shriveled runt that died within hours but once Jane had seen her creep into their neighbour's litter and come skulking back with a calico kitten in her mouth. A week-old half-blind stumbling kitten and she brought it into a closet, made a little nest of a fallen housecoat, and attempted to nurse it. Her father wrestled the kitten back and returned it before trouble broke but what Jane remembers is the sight of Zola with the kitten in her mouth, creeping through the hallway. Her sharp teeth so soft, so tender. Such a vigilance of care. In the end, Jane explains, motes twirling in the slant light of her eight-by-ten room, Zola stopped eating, left red streaks on the basement floor. Jane's father had wanted to put her in the garage and turn the car's engine on, but Jane saw the cat looking out towards the garden that spilled onto a creek, a few wild acres beyond. So they let her outside and she walked into the forest and Jane sat with her father, drinking seltzer with fresh anise. Sat not talking but waiting, thinking about what birds might be circling, the fox she'd seen across the creek last year, the raccoon skull she'd found at the hewn base of a deadfall. Jane tells me how strange it was to find nothing, absolutely nothing the next day when she went and looked by the river. No bones, no fur, no blood, no shit.

"It seemed nice," she said. "To just evaporate into forest. It seemed like a good way." Outside, the groundskeeper turns a hose on, and together we watch the fine mist rise, bloom colours in the sun. Jane turns to me, then back to the window. "Can you help me?"

Her houseplants are dry, roots rising through the soil. "I'm not sure what you mean."

"With dying. Can you help me die?"

I look into her pale eyes, their rinds of cataract. She is calm, serious, resigned.

"I don't know. I don't think so."

"No," she says. "No, of course not."

Then she does something strange. She puts her hand on my stomach and just holds it there. Jane doesn't rub or knead or pet. She just palms my stomach, holds her pale and shivering hand there, cradling my hurt. Eventually, she takes her hand back into her lap, and I walk out among the floral hallways, the smell of tonight's casserole rising up from the kitchen, the rooms full of air conditioners and ventilators, bones and fetid flesh.

FOUR DAYS OFF means thinking about Jane, thinking about insulin, thinking about the virus, about milk poured into pastures, about all the ways a nurse could steward death. I love Ryan, I hate Ryan. Ryan on his morning runs, Ryan bent into his laptop. I sit at the kitchen table staring at a leaf of warped linoleum at the foot of the fridge, where some yogurt from Ryan's breakfast has landed. The linoleum peeling back at the edges, near the base of the counter. Underneath, barely visible, a triangle of clapboard. I call my mother, FaceTime my nurse friends, walk by the closed gyms, the closed parks. Five cases. Four, six. Three deaths. Five. Eight. I scrub my hands. I sanitize my hands. In the living room, Ryan clacks away at emails, Word documents, notes, funding applications. I moisturize my hands. I wash my facemask, launder my six pairs of scrubs. I read that it is not just milk now. It is cadavers, too, the slaughterhouses hotspots for viral transmission and the farmers gassing pigs and cattle in makeshift trailers. Dutch farmers culling mink, pig farmers in Iowa finding new ways to depopulate their livestock. The news is choking ghettos, people dying in hospital hallways, the white rich whining for haircuts and golf. The news is New York City's 7:00 p.m. cheer, Italians singing on balconies. The news is front-line workers, heroes, service. On Facebook, my pediatric nurse friend writes, *This is not a war and I'm not a soldier but I do need PPE thx.* I roll Jane's request over in my mind. I think about airplanes, about forests, about new animals moving into parks, about the hush in the sky. I think about the economy, about the dolphins in the canals of Venice. I clean the fridge, re-pot the plants, trim the maples around the gate. I stare into the pit of despair, a Costco bag clung in a fist of ivy. Around it jungled sumac and ivy and maples, scattered fists of black walnut. The earth drunk with rain, Ryan's tomatoes already flowering. I think about forest bathing, imagine a clotted stream of soupy clover, banks lush with cushion moss, a cat named Zola trying to swim the green current. I do laundry, stare at the cobwebs in the basement, the remains of old washers and dryers hunching in the wet shadows. I imagine an old woman on all fours, crawling naked through a forest, lianas slashing down, a tail furling serpentine from her hindquarters. Her eyes gleaming, vatic, green. In her jaws, something four-limbed, pink-skinned. A slick thing with a vestigial tail, huge eyes fused shut. A thing that could fit in the palm of a hand.

REBECCA: "WE TRIED for so long."

Fatima: "Baby nine weeks now. We're already calling it 'the baby.'"

Luna: "We named the twins. Jaime and Dante."

Rebecca: "Eleven weeks along. Starting to show."

Luna: "We're just not sure if it would work next time—there's no guarantee."

Fatima: "And the money."

Luna: "Sometimes I dream them as a monster, a two-headed thing."

Rebecca: "We can't let him win. We can't let him control us."

Fatima: "But we can have his children?"

Luna: "Double-bind."

Rebecca: "Abomination."

Fatima: "Violation."

Fatima: "All we want to know is why."

I STAND IN FRONT of the supply rack. Three years ago, the news was full of Elizabeth Wettlaufer, the nurse who injected eight elderly long-term care residents with lethal doses of insulin and tried to kill six more. The case was horrific as well as embarrassing for nurses and long-term care facilities. But what I always wondered was why Wettlaufer became a nurse. The media said she was a sociopath but I wonder if it really was just tactical—a way to get close, an opportunity to kill. Or was she, like the rest of us, trying to help people. Trying, in her own way, to care.

Jane regards me as I walk into the room. She doesn't ask why I'm here, or what's in my case. I sit beside her on the bed. She puts her hand on my stomach again. I smell the mould again; realize for the first time it could be coming from her. "Hello," she says simply. I think of all the needy patients on the ward. All the care plans. I think of Ryan, of shards of bone in my fingertips, of the pocked ceiling of the clinic where I felt the vacuum's ire. I think of Rhonda, of my job. I think of all the deaths, the ease of it.

Jane touches my stomach. "It's all right," she says. "Accidents happen."

RYAN SAT WITH me on gleaming pine next to dozens of other wrecked and weeping women. Women who'd met and connected from the Facebook group though I had retreated, wanting quiet, numb, and I was thinking about mixed babies, how they can often look white, especially as newborns. Sometimes they can pass forever. Sometimes they're far lighter than their parents. Sometimes skin tone changes over time. What if we'd never suspected, found out ten, or twenty years later?

Dr. Spencer testified that he believed he was doing a service to humanity. He was a genetically superior individual—tall, fertile, high IQ, free of genetic defects. These women were in need; he had obliged them. A sixty-year-old man with grey curls and poor skin and drugstore reading glasses, he sat smug in the witness box before the sixty-two women whose lives he had gorged, shredded, gnawed. The women he had sworn to help, had violated with an agar plate. At one point our eyes met, just for a moment, and I felt all the contagion of his gaze. I felt his want, his venom and in that moment something grew in me. Something pushed and squirmed, flailed and thrashed and beat the walls.

IN THE MORNING I find Jane's bed vacant and why does the world rock, buckle? I speed-walk to the office but can't get into the files. Rhonda's on a phone call with corporate, her computer locked. I look in the break room and the dining hall and the smoking section by the back dumpsters, but I can't find Jane's PSW. I phone St. Joseph's but they put me on hold so I decide to walk the five minutes. I don't sign out, just head livid and desperate down the hill, approaching the wind-licked street. The sky is grey, traffic lulling down Richmond towards the university.

When I started at Dream Haven, Rhonda told me not to get close and I felt like laughing. Close? That was the furthest thing from the problem. The problem was rage, resentment, bitterness. The problem was flung shit and clutching need and so how is it that now I want her? Now I need this woman with her mountains of excrement, her philosopher cat, her forest bathing. I need her to be all right but here I am in the abandon, everything coming together, everything building as the pink walls rumble by, as I enter the cafeteria and ask who has seen Jane? Who has seen Jane? The teal floors trembling and the smells of this place running thick through the halls as I lean into the wall and squeak down, something sour crawling my throat. The floors gleaming, freshly buffed and the walls pink as tonsils here in the throat of the world, the smell of gravy roiling through the hallway and into my stomach. The bleat of machinery and the sound, from another floor, of someone groaning in pain and I am seeing all the UTIs, all the unguents, all the bedsores and the purpled flesh, all the injections and tests and the rotting flesh and turning the bodies, turning the bodies. The smell of gravy turning into my stomach and the world starting to flex, to tremble, to blur when Rhonda appears and says she's outside. I ask who and she says Jane, she heard I was looking for her, her grandson came.

Outside, there are blue masks littered all over the lawn. Blue masks caught on the fence, fluttering like lost flags, blackened with the marks of yesterday's footsteps. Halfway down the hill I see the hand, the vehicle. A squat blue hatchback, the thin arm waving, beckoning. Approaching the window, I see her grinning. She's wearing sunglasses and a jean jacket. "I've been saved," she sings, jokey. "This is my grandson, Adam. It all happened very fast."

Adam has a thick red beard, eyes a little too close together. "It was too much," he says, putting a hand on his grandmother's shoulder. "We've been so scared. Enough is enough. She's going to come live with us."

I stand on the curb, humbled, harrowed, hollowed, forcing a smile.

"Well," Jane says from the passenger seat. "I guess it's best not to hug."

Adam shrugs, rolls his eyes. "Protocols."

"Take care," Jane says.

I manage a stiff smile, a weary wave. Adam steps on the gas and the blue hatchback zooms quietly down the hill, turns onto Richmond. Jane doesn't turn her head or lean into the window or press her palm against the glass. I stand there on the edge of the hill, traffic whipping by and all the grass cut short, prim, perfectly contained. Watching Jane's window roll up, the hatchback's signal light blinking on, masks trembling in the grass. I would like to tell her about all the things we take in, take on, about all the taking in this care.

THE
EMPATHY PILL

YOU POP OFF, whirl your tiny fists, declare your cat-voiced rage. The pain shrieks through nipple and gland as I bob and rise, rock you to the window, behold the smokewashed dark. Two weeks now—enough to know what soothes you. The lactation consultant told me to count to ten, wince away the pain. Together, we watch the Maglites slur the slumped hills, the scorched fireweed, the breaks and trenches and deadfall. You are poised, alert, clouds and smoke coiling silver in your steel-grey eyes.

We have been told the fire will not come this close to the sea. We have been told to stay inside, that the worry, here, is smoke. In the city, repurposed cruise ships dwarf the docks, their shadows slanting over the harbour walk, the empty hotels, the abandoned hospital, the smouldered bush. The rescue effort funded by Streamline Energy, a million more migrants to run on the mills, feed the mouth of a billion teeth.

I dance you into the kitchen, slide the salt gauze pads into the nursing bra, bite and clench as the sting creeps, flares, snarls. The lactation consultant, who is no longer answering her messages, recommended the gauze along with an APNO cream. This morning I dared a peek in the mirror, beheld a gratin of pus and scab.

Impossibly, you are hungry again. You turn, flailing. Begin to peck, to root. I bounce you against my chest. Coo and purr, head to the bathroom for the Q-tip and gentian violet. Your mouth opens, bleat leaking through the room. I dab the Q-tip and paint my nipples, stain your lips with the latch. I hold you strong but gentle, just below the skull. The pain rises, flexes, rolls, your tongue a blade. The lactation consultant said count to ten, it would be better after ten. I listen for the swallows, ride their dip and rise. You pop off, your lips serrated midnight. Around your stained mouth the skin is pale, nearly lucent. You stretch, a spasm of leg and fist, and meet my eyes. I stare back, stroke your pallid cheeks, kiss the bane of your lips.

LAST YEAR WE SWAM with whale sharks off the Yucatán Peninsula. A dozen of us loaded onto the skiff, revved over the choppy water and out past the artificial reef. The water changed then. Stilled. The guide had told us about the drop-off, but it was another thing to feel it—crossing the plain, the ocean gaping. A change in the darkness, the sea floor ten thousand feet below. We waited for the planes to hum overhead, drop the larvae like confetti on the sea, compel the rise of the ancients.

The guide had watermelon-printed board shorts and a deep tan. He helped us cinch the necklines of our SafeSuits. "Don't chase them," he told us. "Just wait. They choose you." Alice and I dropped together. "Stay calm," the guide said. "And don't forget to breathe."

At first, nothing but black water. At the surface the two of us in our snorkelling gear, the clownish paddles of our feet. Below, the bobbing murk. I looked down into the still black vast, a world of no horizons. Formless, the deep sea brooded.

They came slow and sudden, like dreams from the bottomless beyond. Two Jurassic giants, glowing dimly. The glow—was it real, natural, some trick of the sun? Or was it the effect of the spilled reactor, the Long Weep? Their skin shimmered steel blue, catching sunlight, their great tails stirred the sea. The bigger one came close to me, her blank face the length of my body. She was sleek and curved. I sensed her age like a glitch in time. She opened her mouth. Had she wanted, she could have swallowed me whole. Instead, she let her wet world seep through and out the other side. Her eye met mine, fist-sized and black. She paid no heed and knew me completely, utterly. She knew my insignificance, my powerlessness. She knew my gaping helplessness, the things I can never change.

In the boat afterwards, flushed and giddy, Alice looked at me and shouted over the Zodiak's purr. She touched the little pout of her stomach and said she could not believe it, a thing that was maybe two hundred million years old, that could swim down six thousand feet. We didn't know where they came from, what was down there. Alice said maybe there really was some other place, some place where they could hide, be safe. Some place where there was still food growing, pockets of krill. She asked if she sounded crazy. I told her yes. She sounded crazy and wild, crazy and right.

Back at the hotel room, after dinner, we sat on the patio and watched the moon's trail dance on the slapping waves. We didn't talk, just sat there pondering. I didn't need to ask what she was thinking about; I knew her mind was sliding out past the reefs, to where the world dropped off, where giants hid their secrets in the cold unseen. "I don't know," she said, as if to herself. "It was so strange. I was sure they'd come to save us."

IN THE FLIRT of dawn I bite back the pain. Collect my calm by some drugged wonder. You suckle and twitch your corkscrew tongue. My nipples are pitch-dark now, still stained with last night's violet. In the window, a rotor-whirling locust hovers on the stubbled hills. Ropes furl down, and the Nomex saviours rappel towards the ditch.

My father calls from the jellyfish city, from his room in the Chiliagon, the dome of a thousand eyes. I tell him another hard night. Up five times, or six. I tell him we still have power and running water, that the fire is not meant to reach us. I take my pills and swallow and he asks what I'm drinking, if I've named you yet. I say nothing and no, watching the grey sun rise through the haze above the hills, the helicopter's rotor-wash making a whorl of ember and char.

"Are you getting care?"

"Yes."

"How's Alice?"

"Fine."

How could I speak the truth? In the distance, Nomex guardians trawl the hills, tote their drip-torches. The rotor whirls dirt and ash. From here, the embers look like spores. My father says he's wiring me more money. I tell him I don't need it. I still have income, the computer in the basement, the steady wheeze of its calculations, its endless trades.

"Willow," he says.

"Yes?"

"Are you all right?"

"Yes."

"Are you sure?"

"I'm sure."

"Fine. But you have to get out as soon as you can. Get to the ships."

The scoff sounds mean, beaten. "The ships? To run on the Sustainamills? If we're lucky?"

"Use my ID."

"I don't know. We—I—always said."

He pauses, swallows audibly. "What else is there?"

After he says goodbye, I set you on the altar of the changing pad. The plastic clip has shifted on your stomach, and when I touch it the fastener floats free, trailing the withered slug of your umbilicus. Your navel stares back—a tangled eye. A trace of the rotten cord slicks the bloat of your stomach. I wipe it, leave your core gleaming pink, a brown stain on the wipe. S-shaped, a kind of rune. The last brown weep of her.

AT NIGHT, I HAVE been hearing something in the water at the back of the house. Something calm and large at the end of the dock, the surf slapping against it like the hull of a boat. I have walked alone to the kitchen window, peeked through the blinds. I have seen a great shadow, the size of a submarine, the texture of slime-slick granite. An oval peeking from the water, I can see that it's mostly submerged, the bulk of it hidden by the sea. Out there by the dock the ocean and the air are just layers of shadow and darkness. But the creature's flesh hums through the dark—a seep of violet in the weeping night.

I have longed to walk up the hill, into the fire, the smoulder. The thought itself is remote, a strange throbbing calm. Climbing to the charred fringe, wading the scorched trunks, limbs blackened and peeled. Roots footed in a froth of ash. The canopy crackling in the distance and, closer, the rows of cedar limbs sintering together, the pink petals of fireweed clinging on at the fringe.

YOU STIR IN the night, tug me from sleep. Eyes closed, you clutch and root. In the window, swirls of smoke and moon. Dream-feeding, the lactation consultant called it. I cradle the words as you clamber and latch, thump tiny fists against my fledgling breasts. Dream-feeding. I imagine a creature who feeds on dreams. A tiny neon insect stalking closets and floorboards, sensing the change in the air currents, the flutter of REM.

You swallow, breathe, swallow again. Pop off red-faced and quivering. Eight hairpin hoses wet the sheets. I grab the towel, dab. Compressing the letdown, I latch you on again. You suckle—happy, now, and quiet. I wince against the sting.

My flow is steady, sometimes too fast. The hormones have done well. A dose of progestin a day during pregnancy, then the domperidone. My chest has sprouted into a C-cup, milk ducts taking root in the new tender flesh. Even before she left, this was always the plan. She'd asked why she should do all the feeding and what if she couldn't, what if she had trouble. The literature called the kit an "empathy pill."

As you suckle, I whisper about your mother, a creature of the ocean, a tall lithe woman who led tourists up and down the gorge, beyond the foothills where the land hunches like a great beast, the dry bank winding along its spine. "All of it," she would tell her tourists, "had once been under the sea." Then she would lead them into the cave, plunge with them into azure pools.

You glug and swallow and kick as I tell you how she swam, long tanned arms wheeling, how I was often scared that she'd gone out too far, I couldn't swim with her. But she always came back, a calm, full, animal smile on her lips. A smile only the sea could give her.

After the Weep, she had to do the same tour but with SafeSuits. Full facial. They had models that would simulate marine life, the wet wriggle of sea moss against your heels. She managed five years like that. She managed you. She said what else was there but to go on fighting, hoping, to give you the best life we could.

She had trouble, sometimes, like the rest of us. She had trouble living, she cried watching the fires climb up the gorge. But she did not know that people would flee, that the hospitals would be derelict, that there would be one harried nurse for six labouring mothers, that she would be unable to push you through. "Wide shoulders, small canal," the nurse said as you hissed and howled and squatted and sweated and strained and shrieked, finally, "Cut me, cut me, cut her out." The nurse found someone to hold the forceps as she sliced your mother, pulled you out stun-still and blood-shocked and clamped her closed again. Your fevered glossy mother held you pale and trembling, fearful of the tidal sleep that lapped at the fringe of her. Her eyelids fluttered lethargic as she bit her lip against the fade. The nurse bursting down the hallway shouting, "Transfusion!" getting no answer but hallway echo and distant moan. At the base of the bed a blue bucket of blood, fist-sized clumps floating. Holding you, then, in the generator light, she spoke to you. She told you to be wild, wild as fire, as rain. She said she wanted you to know that it was beautiful, all of it, and it could still be. That you could be beautiful, live beautiful, even in the burn.

I AM NOT FINE Dad I am not fine we are not fine this is not all right I am barely holding on Alice is gone I am alone this is not possible I am weak I am lost she is gone the baby is screaming screaming the baby eating me gnawing me bleeding scarred nipples ruined body eaten by this child for this child there are drugs for the pain the hospitals are empty I don't want the ships floating cities screaming children disease just to run in the basement fuel the Meduselage how long can we make it the world a singed wick a splayed thread alone with this fierce-screaming child eating gnawing thing breathless with scream a factory of need no way to meet the need need need alone with this scalpel-lipped horror alone and ashamed and in love awful sour tender ruined love I am wreckage screams coiled and wretched screams like smoke no time to heal no sleep break drown rage reek tremble shudder burn.

DISTANT SMOKE sashays in your grey eyes when we hear it, a change in the slop of the beach. Something down there. Our visitor. The swaddle cinched around your face, snug above the nose. We walk outside, stand for a moment in the wind-tossed char, then turn towards the sea. We skirt the house and descend the rocks, lit by distant fire and the unseen moon. The air cools as we approach the dock. There is nothing on the beach. The sea throbs and shimmers with reflected flame. A haze of smoke rests over the water.

My toes slip into the cool, the water lit orange. In the distance, we can see the slurred shadows of the hulking ships. Sea-bound cities, full of vomit and pain.

The first night I slept with you she sent me a dream. We were climbing a road made of rainbows through a hazy night sky. Alice was there, though her face was featureless, void. You were in my arms, suckling sweet and painless. We were climbing towards a fissured moon with scars in its surface, deep jagged cracks. As we climbed, two whale sharks swam towards us. Their faces were blank, massive. Their eyes were black pebbles in the sides of their heads. *Don't worry*, the sharks whispered. *This will pass, one way or another. You are but motes in the eye of time.* Ahead of us, the moon darkened, bloomed cracks, became snarled and snagged, seemed to pulse and glow. Around those fissures the moon had turned a deep violet, darker than blood.

When she appears, dark on dark in the parting sea, you are not alarmed by the bulk of her. You do not tremble as the waves slap her stone-wet skin. Your eyes are wide open, totally alert. You extend a quivering arm towards her, the taut bundle of your fist. The waves slop the curved monument of her back. She is huge, wet, rising, releasing. You cling to me, clear-eyed and calm, gaze fixed on the slick of her back. She flicks her tail, holding still in the hazy shallows. Beyond the point, smoke gives way to mist. She floats in the softly sobbing sea, rudders her tail. You reach for her, the petals of your fingers peeling open for the first time. The sea beneath us changes colour, blooms new shades of black.

ACKNOWLEDGEMENTS

THESE STORIES WERE written on the lands of the Anishinaabek, Haudenosaunee, Lūnaapéewak, Attawandaron, Mi'kmaq, and Wolastoqiyik. The active treaties are the London Township and Sombra Treaties of 1796, the Dish with One Spoon Covenant Wampum, and the Peace and Friendship Treaties. I thank the people, the animals, the plants, the water, and the living land.

Thanks to John Metcalf, tireless editor and visionary mentor; Dan Wells and all the fine folks at Biblioasis; my talented and steadfast agent, Stephanie Sinclair; historian David D. Plain, who consulted on settler-Indigenous relations and history in Lambton County. Thanks to Jen and Taylor for their expertise; to the two anonymous Imperial Oil employees who gave interviews; to David Edwards, for refinery stories; to Monica Virtue, for consulting; to the two anonymous nurses who spoke to me in spring 2020.

Earlier versions of these stories appeared in *The Fiddlehead*, *The New Quarterly*, EVENT, *Best Canadian Stories 2018*,

The Journey Prize Stories 32, *long con magazine*, and *Canadian Notes & Queries*. My deep thanks to the handling editors— Shashi Bhat, Anita Chong, Emily Donaldson, Mark Anthony Jarman, Pamela Mulloy, Kailee Wakeman, and Andy Verboom—and the editorial teams that poured care into my work. "Six Six Two Fifty" was nominated for the 2019 National Magazine Award in fiction. "Chemical Valley" was a finalist for the 2020 Journey Prize. I am grateful to the readers and jurors.

The creation of this manuscript was supported by funding from the Canada Council for the Arts, the London Arts Council, and the Ontario Arts Council. I finished this book while working as the 2020–2021 writer-in-residence at the University of New Brunswick. My sincere thanks to Sue Sinclair for her keen and steady guidance, and to all the lovely people I met through UNB.

Thanks, also, to my readers: Natasha Bastien, Chris Benjamin, Tom Cull, Blair Trewartha, and Aaron Kreuter. Thanks to the Hueberts, the Edwardses, Les Bastiens, and to Rose and Sybille, who daily bend my world.